TODAY, TOMORROW & FOREVER

A Novel

By

Alexandra Y. Caluen

TODAY, TOMORROW & FOREVER

The Playlist:

Too Close for Comfort - Frank Sinatra

Uptown Girl - Billy Joel

Stop Drop & Roll - Squirrel Nut Zippers

Beggin' - Madcon

Kryptonite - 3 Doors Down

So Far Away - Avenged Sevenfold

Ordinary World - Duran Duran

Afterglow - INXS

River of Dreams - Billy Joel

Fishies – The Cat Empire

El Matador - Los Fabulosos Cadillacs

TODAY, TOMORROW AND FOREVER

Contents

I - Grace
October 2015

I was at Mom's house that day because we had a plan to do dinner together, the three of us. I'd gone to see her boyfriend Ray in the 'Gaucho' show and we all wanted to do a post-show get-together, but with my classes and everything, that month after the show closed was a mess. I hadn't seen either of them, except at the show, for six weeks. As it turned out, Mom wasn't even home when I got there. She'd texted me to say she was working at the studio with a student who was entered at the Hollywood DanceSport Championships (a local ballroom competition) and was already freaking out, and apparently the talk-him-off-the-ledge was taking some extra time.

So I let myself in and went to the kitchen, because there was usually something good to eat in there, and my incoming-senior-year schedule had not left me with much time or inclination to feed myself in ways that went beyond 'drive through.' I could hear music coming from Mom's practice room as soon as I got in the house, and assumed Ray was back there working on something. Then, while I was raiding the refrigerator, I heard two men laugh and thought *huh*.

I knew Ray regularly had friends over. Now that he was playing a cop full-time on 'Ten-31' and doing Latin competition with Mom, he never went out on calls as an extra, but he knew a lot of people from those days and he kept in touch with them. Then I heard him laugh again and say "No, God no, Lucas please stop," and the other guy straight-up giggled. It made me smile.

The music was still going, but after a minute I heard footsteps and could tell they were coming through to the kitchen. I'll confess, I was curious. Most of Ray's friends were men who were - naturally - close to his age, which made them a little bit old for me (though, given Ray was sixteen years younger than Mom, the whole age thing was kind of a non-issue in our family). But most of his friends also seemed to be hella cute, so, you know, well worth seeing regardless. Even the lawyer dude was good-looking.

Anyway, knowing they were en route, as it were, I made sure I wasn't actively chewing anything and prepared to be entertained. I kept my back to the doorway, so I could be oh-so-casually surprised when they came in.

"Oh hey Gracie," said Ray behind me. "I didn't hear you come in. We've got dinner tonight, right?"

I turned around, looking at Ray – he may have been Mom's, but I still knew exactly where he was in a room; he was that kind of guy – and said, "Yeah, I was ahead of things for a minute so I came over early. How you doing?"

"I'm good," he said. "This is my buddy Lucas. Lucas, this is Julia's daughter Grace. She's a senior at USC."

"Hey Grace, nice to meet you," said the other guy as I turned my head to look at him. He held out a hand, and I took it mechanically, trying to maintain the casual thing, but thinking *holy hell he looks like Fifties Elvis*, which just so you know is a very good thing in my opinion. We shook hands and I let go, thinking I was doing pretty well with my poker face. He asked, "Are you a dancer, too?"

"I *can* dance," I said. "I *have* danced. Mom and Ray insist on it. But I'm in school to be an engineer."

"Ray's trying to teach me salsa," he said. "My agent put me up for an audition that we both thought was hip-hop, and then we get the sheet and it says salsa." His voice was much like Ray's, a mellow baritone, or in other words ideal.

"He was crying to me on the phone the next minute," said Ray with that face that guys do with their guy friends sometimes, a mix of mockery and affection. I laughed. Lucas shrugged, eyebrows up, like *well yeah*, and Ray added, "The audition's tomorrow."

"Then you'd better get back to work," I said. I liked that he was the kind of guy who took that situation as a challenge, and not as a reason to say oh, not this time I guess.

"But we're hungry." Ray went to the refrigerator like I had, peered into it like I had, and pulled out about six things, handing them back to Lucas. I stood there and watched, leaning against the counter out of their way, while they put together their snack, because those two guys moving around were fun to watch. Lucas wasn't quite Ray's height but had a similar build (let's call it athletic), and was – I was pretty sure - Latino; his skin was a couple of shades lighter than Ray's and his hair was glossy black.

"So what have I seen you in?" I asked Lucas, assuming I would have seen him in something during the multi-year Find Ray Film Festival that Mom and I had indulged in. He mentioned a couple of things, and I made a mental note to go back and look for him.

Then he added, "Plus me and my boys came in second one year on America's Best Dance Crew."

"Hey, good job," I said, impressed. "I love that show."

He smiled, this shy proud thing that just about killed me. "It was good for us. We got a sponsor for a year to do competition all over the world. Then I got a gig in Vegas, worked out there a few years before coming back to town."

"The rest of his crew went out on a U.S. performance and teaching tour," said Ray. "They ended up leaving people behind all over the place. It was only the one guy who came back here, right?" He looked at Lucas, who nodded.

"Yeah. Couple guys stayed in Miami, one guy stayed in Dallas, one guy went to Seattle and all we still hear from him is whining about the rain. We're all, dude, it's Seattle, what did you expect."

I laughed again. "Why does he stay?"

"Met a girl." Lucas shrugged. "A man will put up with a lot."

It looked like Ray wanted to add something to that, but all he said was, "So Grace, would you do us a favor and help me demo some stuff? He picked up the basics fast, but for the leads, it's hard to demonstrate both parts at once."

"Sure," I said, because there wasn't much I could think of that would be more fun than dancing with these guys. It certainly topped my other waiting-for-Mom option of watching TV. "I've got some dance shoes upstairs."

"Cool. See you out back in a few. Come on, brother." Ray and Lucas went out, and I cleaned up the kitchen (rolling my eyes) before going up to the room still designated as Mine. It was tempting to put on something other than jeans and a tee shirt, but I thought that would be too obvious, so it was just the shoes, ma'am, and I went back to the practice room.

They were running basics when I got there, which reinforced my impression that Lucas was like Ray: a guy who did the work. Maybe it was a function of age, but I hadn't met a lot of guys so far – guys my own age, that is - who didn't give off a faint aroma of entitlement. But, I reminded myself, this was allegedly a dance lesson and I should be serious because the guy was trying to get a job, not trying to get a date. So I got in line and warmed up by doing the salsa basics with them.

Within five minutes I could tell that Lucas had rhythm, was placing his feet correctly, and didn't seem to be having any trouble with the various basics; he was following along with Ray with no visible hesitation. Ray apparently agreed, because without a word beyond "Okay let's do this" he took me into dance hold and started doing all those same basics. Lucas stood back and watched; this part must have been obvious by now, since all a follower did in the basics was the natural opposite of what the leader did.

Then Ray started really leading, and I had to pay more attention, but I could tell that Lucas got focused. Ray was sort of narrating the process, about how changing his own body angles would change the shape of something, or open up a path for me to do something. What 'outside partner' meant, and 'cross-body.' How the inside and outside turns worked. How to lead a check - a movement where the follower was stopped, usually in some kind of eye-catching pose - or a drop or a few other simple tricks. I was sweating when he finally stopped.

When I glanced at the clock I was startled to see that nearly an hour had passed. "Damn," I said, "no wonder I'm tired." Both men laughed. Ray did not look nearly as worn-out as I felt. "I'm out of shape!"

"You're studying other stuff," said Ray forgivingly. "This is pretty much all we do these days, is work out."

"Yeah," said Lucas. He went over to the wet bar Mom had installed, and got me a glass of water.

"Thanks." I gulped it down. "Whew."

"So how much of that do you think you got?" Ray asked Lucas, somewhat challengingly. I wondered what he was up to. Maybe this was just part of their dynamic. I mean, I knew there was generally a good bit of chops-busting anytime two guys were in a room.

Lucas didn't say anything, only shook his head with a little smile, like 'I got this,' and held out his hand. I went over to him, not expecting much. Ray had left the music playing, and it was right in the middle of a song. Lucas started doing all those basics as if he'd been doing them all his life. Then the song changed, and he kept dancing, adjusting to the new tempo and style, and started doing the different figures.

I'd been kind of avoiding his eye, because it's always awkward - almost embarrassing - to make eye contact with someone you hardly know, especially when you're only, like, a foot away from them. But when he started doing combinations that I knew damn well Ray hadn't shown him a few minutes ago I looked up. I might have been frowning a little; it was a habit, one Mom said she used to have BB (before Botox), and it didn't usually mean anything, but Lucas asked, "This okay?" I nodded, and he kept dancing, but now we were looking at each other.

I'll tell you what I liked about it. First of all, he didn't push. A lot of guys (especially beginners) push you around. It's obnoxious, and actually makes it harder to follow because the follower is supposed to go (for the most part) where the leader's *body* goes, not where his

6

hand goes. Anyway, there was that. Second, his posture was good. That was a surprise because hip-hop tends to be kind of low and, well, funky. Social-dancing posture always needs to be upright, and his was. Third, his hold was light but his frame was solid. He didn't squeeze my hand too hard and he didn't bounce his arms around. It was seriously one of the best dance experiences I'd had that wasn't with Ray.

Also, of course, he was exactly the height I preferred a dance partner to be, and he looked like Elvis. What the hell was I supposed to not like?

After enough time had passed that I was starting to notice my feet (getting sore, that is), the music stopped. So did Lucas, letting go of me and stepping away. I kind of stood there trying to catch my breath. I glanced over at Ray, by the music setup, and he was looking at the LCD screen of his camera. I hadn't been paying any attention to what he was doing. "Were you taping that?"

"Yeah," he said. "Okay if I send it to my boy to review at home?"

After a second I said, "Sure," because why not, though I was dying to see it myself. Then I said recklessly, "Send it to me, too." He smiled a little, but his eyes narrowed, as if there was something he wanted to say. I did this thing he showed me, this thing that says *WHAT ARE YOU NOT SAYING* without actually speaking out loud; it's one of the few acting tricks he'd taught me that has stuck, maybe because I do it all the time. Anyway, he clearly got the message but he didn't say anything else, only looked over at Lucas in a way that sent a different message. I turned my head. "Was that really your first time dancing salsa with a partner?"

Lucas said, "Salsa, yeah. I've done some other stuff." He wasn't looking at me, though; he was looking at Ray, and there was a whole conversation happening. Then he closed his eyes for a second and took a visibly deep breath, turned to me with a practiced smile and said, "I've only had one round of real social-dance lessons. My wife wanted us to do a waltz at our wedding."

Oh, I thought. His wife. Okay.

I put my poker face back on, said something about how I hoped he got the job, and I enjoyed working with him. Then I glared daggers at Ray and calmly, collectedly fled the scene.

At dinner that night Ray told Mom that Lucas had come over and I'd helped out with a salsa lesson. Mom only nodded. Either she hadn't met Lucas, or she had met him and hadn't really noticed him because Ray was in the room (which is, in my opinion, how it should be when you're in love with somebody), or she had met him and he hadn't made an impression. I didn't think that was it. But in any case, Ray didn't embarrass me, and I didn't embarrass myself, though I did make a joke about being out of shape and needing to hook up with the USC ballroom club so I wouldn't acquire a Senior Muffin-Top.

I usually stayed overnight when I came for dinner now that I was twenty-one and Mom could ply me with alcohol. (Not really. She'd been letting me have a glass of wine with dinner since I was a freshman, but now that I was legal if I topped up my glass she didn't take it away from me.) That night after I helped clean up the kitchen (again) I went up to my room as usual. Instead of getting ready for bed I kind of flopped across it and stared at the ceiling.

I was talking to myself – inside my head, I assure you – a thing I do maybe more than I should, but I'd been living alone since transferring out of Santa Monica

College and who else was I going to discuss things with? In this case, I was interrogating myself about why a couple of hours of dancing had so effectively shut down my natural, and honed-to-razor-edge, tendency to Analyze. Because Ray was how old he was, and it was highly likely that Lucas was also about ten years older than me, and it was always going to be completely unlikely that a guy who looked like that, who was making a living in the industry, and who was actually nice, was also single. So why, I had to ask myself, had I not asked myself that question at any time after turning around and seeing his face?

Because that was usually the *first* question I asked myself. And this time instead of my usually-helpful brain producing Is He Single, Because Damn, my totally-unhelpful brain had produced something best rendered as Yum.

Yumbody else's man. Damn it.

After a while I heard Mom and Ray coming up the stairs, so I sat up and tried to look like I was reading the random book that had been on the nightstand. Ray went down the hall to the master bedroom. Mom stopped at my door. I glanced up, oh so casually. "Hi Mom."

"Hi honey. Want to talk about it?"

Oh shit, I thought. Surely Ray didn't rat me out. My face must have said that – when I didn't consciously do Poker Face it was kind of Obvious Face – because she shook her head. I set down the book and beckoned her in; she closed the door behind her. "Knocked for a loop," I said bluntly, because, thank God, we could really talk to each other. She knew all about my previous crushes, infatuations, and other adolescent love affairs. "But he's married, so that's that. I'm processing, whatever."

"I'm sorry," she said.

"It was bound to happen sometime. At least it was here at home with Ray around to supervise." And seriously, what a blessing that was.

"What's your strategy?"

I must have looked surprised, because she laughed a little. "I don't have a strategy. I'm going to go back to school and do what I do. The world is full of inappropriate men, it's dumb luck that I haven't wanted one before. I'll get over it. I'll be okay."

"I know you will." She came over to the bed, bent down, and kissed me on the forehead. "Good night, honey."

"Good night, mom." That little kiss, I swear, she almost had me going. But I held it together. It was just a dance lesson, after all.

You keep telling yourself that, Gracie, my brain said to me. *Where were you when I needed you*, I said to my brain.

I - Lucas
December 2015

I don't remember what I thought when I first saw her that day, except 'Thank God I'm married,' which might be a weird thing to think when you've been introduced to somebody that beautiful. She looked a lot like her mother, actually, which was a good thing. And a bad thing, because it was all too easy to imagine how she would look in thirty-whatever years: still beautiful. But way out of my league. White girl, engineer, big-ass West L.A. house, and I knew her dad was some big-shot lawyer.

Of course, by the second or third song, or minute, of dancing with her I was thinking pretty clearly 'too bad I'm married,' which is a scary thing to think. Not that I hadn't thought it before, a bunch of times, and not that I hadn't been thinking it more and more often recently. Sharysse looked so indifferent, now, whenever I got home from a trip or a gig. She didn't ever act excited to see me anymore. Or even pleased, really. It was almost like I was inconveniencing her by being home. Half the time I pretended I didn't notice and everything was fine, half the time I tried to be all happy and lovey, like we were brand-new again, or like we were when we first got married.

Anyway, in the moment I wished Ray had minded his own business, because I'm a grown man and Grace is a grown woman. But in the next moment I was so grateful that he gave me that signal, that look that said 'shut it down now.' Because she didn't deserve to be misled for even a minute, and I could tell that she liked me too. Just from the way she danced, if nothing else.

But I've always been pretty good at distinguishing genuine interest from polite interest. Grace's blue eyes were sharp and intelligent, and the way she'd studied me hadn't been polite. Her body was strong and well-trained, and the way she'd moved with me had been real. If Ray hadn't been in the room I might have tried a thing I used to do in the clubs, when my boys and I would go out to dance bachata and merengue, a little trick that let us get our hands in a girl's hair. Grace's hair was brown, not black like most of the girls I'd known, and silky-smooth, and cut to fall straight to her shoulders. With her dance shoes on, she was only a couple inches shorter than me. I'd had plenty of time to study those eyes, and the shape of her face, and the way her lips parted, turning up a little, when I gave her a double turn.

So I reviewed that video when I got home, and if every other time through I was looking more at Grace than at myself, well, a man's not made of stone. I went to the audition the next afternoon, and when they actually taught a short class before having people couple up for the casting director, I realized how far ahead those few hours with Ray and Grace had put me. Instead of floundering through it like some of the guys, I knew the language and I knew what it should look like.

I got the gig. A month later I was over in Las Vegas to shoot, and they'd moved me from special-skills extra to bit player, with just a dozen lines but spread over three scenes. It really gave me a chance to make an impression using my words, as they say. The extras wrangler told me, after the second day, that someone had floated the idea of making my character an Elvis impersonator.

It made me laugh, but I sure would have done it if they'd gone for it. They might even have let me sing. I was going on thirty and it was time to see if this less-painful branch of the business was going to work out … or if I needed to invest in Advil and get back in training to perform and teach hip-hop. I mean, there's only one

Twitch. The rest of us have to be out on the road breaking our backs and putting together routines to submit to 'So You Think,' because Christopher Scott ain't the only player with an idea. And I'll be straight with you: that show is the way to go if you want to get recognized as a choreographer, so it was always in the back of my mind, but still. Dancing for hours every day will beat you down. I was the only guy in my old crew who hadn't broken a bone. Yet.

Once the shoot wrapped and I was on my way home, I emailed Ray a bit of video that a new buddy took of an after-hours rehearsal, where I did a little bit of dancing and then my little bit of dialogue with an actress playing a cocktail waitress. Looking it over, I thought the salsa was legit, so I was happy. And I wrote *Thank Grace for me, would you? That was a great lesson from start to finish. Definitely would not have landed this gig without it!*

He wrote back a couple days later. Actually, he copied me on his message forwarding the video to Grace. I didn't know what to think. I mean, if he hadn't been around to help put the brakes on we could have been on a slippery slope pretty damn fast. But having someone's email address when you're not supposed to be on *any* kind of slope? It wasn't quite as bad as having someone's phone number. I mean, it's awfully easy to drunk-text somebody. #BeenThereDoneThat. Email is a little more involved. I'd have to really try, is what I'm saying.

I did not send her an email. She didn't send me an email. But there was something almost comforting about knowing she had my address. He'd never said my last name and neither had I, but now she had it. Now she could find out whatever she wanted to about me. If she wanted to. If she hadn't brushed it off, the way I couldn't seem to.

At the end of the year I got a call from Rita, that extras wrangler. She told me she was working on casting a series of commercials for a liquor company and did I want to be on the list. I was like, sure. "And anything else you've got," I added. "I have this feeling I might be having an acting moment. Not sure why."

"Was that the first time you were given lines?"

"Yeah, it was. Maybe all those classes are paying off." Which was not a joke. A special-skills extra gets paid more than a basic background person, but once you start doing lines your rates go up and a SAG card starts looking like a strong possibility. I'd been taking classes for years.

She called me again right after the first of the year. "Hey Lucas, it's Rita. I talked to your agent a few minutes ago. Check your email."

"What's up?"

"Nope, talk to Raquel, I'm not supposed to tell you about it."

"Am I in trouble?"

"Kind of the opposite, I think. Talk to you soon." She hung up, and I went and dug my laptop out of my bag. I'd just gotten home from a thing and I was tired, and a little freaked out because Sharysse wasn't there and hadn't left a note and hadn't texted or called (and hadn't answered *my* texts and calls) so I didn't know where she was. But 'kind of the opposite of in trouble' was working on me, so I booted up and logged on, and found the email from Raquel.

It was every bit worth the tease from Rita, even the second and third times I read it through.

Hey Lucas, I'm hearing good things from the booze folks. They sent me something for you but it's in a bottle so get over here fast. Anyway the people running that shoot in November got back to me about a new thing. They've been hired to produce thirteen episodes for streaming, the project is called 'Behind the Strip' and it's like a soap opera about performers and stage workers in Las Vegas. Lots of sex and drugs and drama I'm assuming (haven't seen a script yet). They want you to come in and read for a part, an Elvis impersonator. You can sing, right? Get back to me ASAP.
Cheers - Raquel

I sat back from the computer, not sure whether I wanted to laugh or cry or scream. This was so close to best case scenario that I felt like there had to be a catch. Of course, like always, the catch was I had to ace the audition. I took my time composing a reply.

Hey Raquel, that's some really interesting news. I'd love to read for the Vegas thing. When can they get me the sides? What kind of song should I prepare? I haven't really done Elvis since high school but you better believe I'll brush that up soonest. And oh yeah - is this hush-hush or could I take it to Ray for some advice?
Thanks - Lucas

p.s. You go ahead and open that bottle :-)

I got an answer in a couple of days. Heard it land in my in-box (my email alert was currently a turkey gobble, not sure why but I still thought it was funny after hearing it about a million times) while I was in the middle of a fight with Sharysse. We'd been fighting more or less nonstop since she finally got home, near midnight the day I'd gotten back. It seemed like every time I managed to shut it down she found a reason to start back up again.

"What is going on?" I finally said, a little bit loud, because she kept bitching about stuff that happened five years ago and I needed to know what the hell was wrong *now*. She stopped talking; I guess my tone made an impression. I was standing all the way across the room from her, as I usually did when we got into it, because she told me once that she hated it when I loomed over her. (I'm not super tall, five eleven, but that's still eight inches taller than her.) She wrapped her arms tightly around herself and didn't say anything for a minute. "Sharysse, what is happening? What are you mad about? What can I do?"

She still didn't say anything. Staring at her, watching her avoid making eye contact, I started to think this wasn't actually about me at all. Now, like any guy with a healthy ego, I automatically assume that everything's about me. Yeah, I said it. But the more I thought about the past couple of days, in that lengthening silence, I thought *she is looking for a way out. She is trying to blast a hole in this wall I've been trying to repair, the wall that used to hold our love in*, and I said, "You're in love with somebody else, aren't you." It wasn't even a question.

And she *still* didn't say anything, but she hugged herself even tighter, and tears started to run down her face.

"I remember when you were happy for me when I got a gig. You said my success was our success." My voice sounded funny, maybe because my throat felt tight. "Now you're just happy because I won't be here." Still not a word. I swallowed hard, took a deep breath or two, thought my voice wouldn't shake when I spoke again, but I was wrong. "I really loved you."

She said "Oh God," and hurled herself across the room and into my arms, sobbing, saying "I'm sorry, I'm so sorry, I didn't mean for this to happen, oh Lucas I'm so sorry."

"It's okay," I kind of whispered, and then just held her, with my face against her hair, blinking hard but not quite managing to stop my tears.

We finally talked, quietly and seriously, a little later. I was right, she'd met somebody else, one of those times I was away. He wanted to marry her. He wanted to have children with her, something that I'd resisted.

And the truth was, when I said *loved* that's what I meant. I'd always care about her, because how can you not care about someone you loved enough to marry? But it was past tense. And saying that, watching her hear it, I could tell it was as much a relief for her as it was for me. It took a layer of guilt off. For her, because she was already in a new thing and it would have been tarnished even worse if she'd known I was still in love with her. For me, well, because of Grace. Because of that little episode when I got a contact high from someone who really dug me.

And now I could admit it. I could admit how badly I'd needed to feel wanted. Even though we hadn't verbalized, much less acted on it. So when Sharysse kind of offered to take me to bed, I had enough pride to thank her nicely and decline. The Grace thing probably would never have gone anywhere, but the next time I went to bed with somebody it was going to be with someone who really wanted me, not someone who only wanted to say she was sorry.

After she went to sleep, even though it was really late, I got on the computer to see what that email said. I'll admit I thought that if I got a job in Vegas now it wasn't going to start a fight, and in spite of everything I almost laughed.

> Hey Lucas, sides are attached. They're seeing people next Monday and Tuesday. Can you prep 'Love Me Tender' and 'Jailhouse Rock'? They'll have backing tracks. Call it audition karaoke. Let me know which day works better for you. Btw fine to discuss with Ray but not with TMZ plz. Grow some sideburns.
> Cheers - Raquel
> p.s. The bottle is open.

I had to put a hand over my mouth to stifle the laugh over the sideburns, the way she threw that in there. I figured I could probably show off a decent set if I asked to be seen on the Tuesday. So I sent back a reply that was basically all 'yes,' then got ready for bed. Meaning the couch. Good thing we chose it for crashing-out comfort.

I talked to Ray over the weekend, mostly about the audition, but found myself telling him about Sharysse. "We're probably getting a divorce," I said, and hearing it out loud – because she and I had not yet said the word – made it horribly real. "She's met someone else."

"Ooh brother," he said softly, with real sympathy in his voice. "I'm sorry to hear that. How you doing?"

"Not great. But not terrible. We had a good talk. Overdue."

"Still, that's a tough one. What's the next step?"

"We'll talk some more, and start the ball rolling, I guess. If this audition works out I'll be in Vegas for a while. Don't want to leave it hanging."

"Yeah. Well listen, keep me posted. Call me anytime."

"I'll do that. Thanks."

The next Tuesday I rolled up to this office suite in Alhambra, God knows how the producers ever heard of it, and found myself waiting along with half a dozen other guys. We all looked more or less like Elvis, but the age range was impressive. I was right in the middle of the pack between a couple guys who didn't even look twenty-one, and a couple more who were clearly fortyish and sixtyish. Several of them were in costume, and one of the young guys had a guitar. I was wearing blue jeans with a white tee shirt and a black leather jacket, hoping that was good enough. We all had black hair but I couldn't swear everyone's was naturally black. I wouldn't even swear it was all natural hair. I was feeling a little nervous, which made me giggly, which was super inappropriate, so I tried to concentrate on the script that they'd provided, even though I already had it memorized.

It seemed like they saw us in age order, ascending. I felt bad for the oldest guy when it was my turn to go in; we'd already all been there for a couple of hours, and the person herding us around had looked annoyed the last time that guy went down the hall to the bathroom.

They asked me a few questions about myself and my background, asked if I could dance. I thought *don't they know?* but answered politely that yes, I could, and that I'd been doing choreography for over ten years. They asked if I could play guitar, and I said, "I played some in high school, but I never had my own." One of them nodded and made a check mark on one of the papers on her clipboard. I was wincing a little inside, thinking that might be a deal-breaker, but they hadn't *asked* for guitar so maybe it wasn't.

They asked me about the previous Vegas shoot, and I came up with a couple of funny stories that flattered the producers. Then they had me do the scene. The person reading the other half of the dialogue was flat as hell, but maybe that was part of the test. I'd studied it, and made up my own rationale for the lines. God knows if I got it right. Finally after talking together for a minute they asked me to do 'Love Me Tender.' I dug deep and channeled the King, but I didn't play it for laughs. I sang it as if Sharysse was there with me and there was still a chance for us. As I finished, I saw one of the production people wiping her eyes, and thought *yeah*.

I had to wait a week for the official word, but I'd already sent an email to Raquel saying I thought I was going to get it. When she finally got back to me all the message said was THANK YOU, THANK YOU VERY MUCH.

A few minutes later a longer message came in with all the details of the offer, but I was still laughing over the first one.

The next day after Sharysse got home from work, we sat down and talked about divorce. Neither of us wanted to make trouble. Neither of us had gone into the marriage with anything. I didn't want any of her money, she didn't want any of mine. Her new guy had been asking her to move in with him, and where he lived worked for her, so she'd simply move out of our apartment and into his. She'd called up a friend who had a lawyer friend who did simple divorces, and gotten that number. We made an appointment to do the paperwork in two weeks. It was all easy.

It was still hard. It's one thing to work hard for what you get, but I wasn't used to failing. I wasn't that guy who would say fine, didn't want you anyway, and walk off like it was nothing. I was also not that guy who would call up his friends and talk about his feelings. So even though Ray made that offer, and I knew he was far enough in love that he would understand, he was also the guy who knew there was that moment with Grace. I couldn't talk to him about how it felt to be left behind. Couldn't talk to anybody. Had to just suck it up and get on with the job.

II - Grace
March 2016

I couldn't figure out why Ray had forwarded that whole email, and not only the video. Or, when it came right down to it, why he hadn't simply said 'Lucas says thanks, he got the job,' and left it at that. Was he maybe subconsciously in favor of me having a thing for his buddy? His *married* buddy? Because I knew Mom would have told him what I'd said, they told each other anything and everything. The only reason that didn't piss me off was that neither of them ever mentioned it to me.

But something still pissed me off a little. Because I was really seriously opposed to even the bare notion of being a homewrecker. I'd brushed off a lot of approaches from married men, sort-of-married men, almost-not-married men. You wouldn't believe how many guys are "separated" or "almost divorced" or "not in an exclusive relationship." And this was all coming to me, a geeky and not-very-remarkable college student in a town full of fully-remarkable actresses and models. God knows what *those* girls had to deal with.

Anyway, that little question wasn't very present in my mind most of the time, because I had enough on my mind with my classes. The amount of mental work I had to do was exhausting. Exciting, too; it was always great to work out a problem or come up with a solution, because every time it was confirmation that I was on the right track, that this career path was right for me. Which was good, because graduation was coming right up.

But yeah: tired. I'd also had to travel for an interview for a summer internship, which put me a little behind, if only in my own mind. And as usual, the thing I squeezed out to the edges of life was people. All the way through fall semester, I kept meaning to go out and

22

do things. I was living downtown, not far from campus, and there are a ton of things to do. I knew a gazillion people in my program, I still had friends I kept in touch with from high school and SMC, but somehow it didn't happen. When I looked back on the holiday break (because Mom asked "What happened with that guy you were seeing last spring?") I realized I hadn't gone out on a single date. And not for lack of offers, really; it was for mutual failure to follow through.

A female engineering student is not as rare as she used to be, but the ratio was a little unbalanced. That said, every senior-year engineering student I knew was unbalanced. The pre-med people were worse. We were all busy. We were not hanging around in bars, or (more likely given who we were) in the public areas at the Natural History Museum, looking for somebody to help us fill up empty hours. Not this year. We were also not cruising the halls looking for someone more appealing than the others in our particular discipline, the ones we saw all the time and had already at least gone to get coffee with unless we found each other completely repugnant. When we got together at all, it was generally to study. Those groups were mixed-gender but they were kind of the opposite of dates.

Anyway, over the holiday break I swore to do better, because no woman is an island, and I could not reasonably expect the men in my peer group to look like the men in Ray's peer group. It was nobody's fault that nobody looked like Lucas. I had to admit (if only to myself) that he was now kind of my dream guy. Smart, hard-working, talented, amazingly good-looking, and nice. Did I have proof that he was smart? Not really. But the way he approached that dance lesson was smart, so I made an assumption. Because I liked him. I refuse to believe I'm the only girl who ever did something like that, and at least it was in the privacy of my own head, because I certainly didn't talk about him.

I distracted myself by calling up my friend Miguel, who wasn't coming home for the holidays for about a million reasons. He'd scored a transfer from Santa Monica College to a university in the Bay Area. That was only even possible because of Ray, who'd decided to do a big-brother thing when I was a sophomore and Miguel was my roommate. I did not honestly miss being crammed together into a studio apartment, but I did miss Miguel. We got really close really fast, and then BOOM he was gone. Off to bigger and better things. I know for a fact Mom wished he wasn't gay, for a while there at least. Then she settled down to being happy that I had an adopted brother. The two of us did not feel the need to fill her in on his adventures in NorCal. Let's say the far-superior public transit up there made some adventures possible that he never got to have in Los Angeles, and leave it at that. I had to make up some ridiculous story to account for the way I was giggling on the phone with him at Christmas.

And then it was back to work. I did slightly better at the social-life thing. The odd meetup here and there, mostly because here in the homestretch I was finding that if I didn't step completely away for a few hours occasionally, my brain started feeling like a TV screen full of static. But I did it mostly as a Maintain Normal Functioning measure, not because I was really trying to form a connection. Mom expressed concern that I was not enjoying my last year of school. She was not a super-old-fashioned woman but I knew 'enjoying myself' was code for 'dating' so I went through the motions. Dating simply seemed like the least-important thing in the world.

If I'd been living at home things might have been different, because something I've noticed is that whatever your routine is, it's self-reinforcing. My routine did not have 'go on an actual date once a week' penciled in. It didn't even have 'go to dinner and speak with fellow human' penciled in. It was a palimpsest of research and writing and test deadlines, written in four fluorescent colors. If I managed to have lunch or coffee or a drink with someone and not mention stress, shear, and load, I considered it an achievement.

That last semester I basically only saw Mom and Ray when they were both doing a show at Chrome - the Sunday night shows made that possible, because my Monday classes didn't start till after noon. I could spend the whole weekend studying or doing assignments, go up to Hollywood on Sunday night, have pizza or something after the show with them, and then go back to my apartment near campus to crash.

They did a number I really liked for the March show, which was all waltzes. They used a mariachi song that was kind of dreamy and sweet even though it was fast, and did a thing they told me was Latin waltz. It looked like salsa in three-quarter time, and of course it made me think of Lucas again, which I trust was not the intention. I never asked about him and Ray never volunteered any information - usually.

Over pizza after the show, we were talking about their next performance and competition plans, and he said, "Alison confirmed she's going with martial arts for the pro show this summer. Danny and Kate are on board to teach everyone katas, Sam and Mateo are helping pick music and start structuring the group routines. Sam and Mary are going to be the leads this time. The auditions for the troupe are next week, I'm going to try out."

"That's cool," I said. "You'll totally get in. You've done martial arts stuff before, right?"

"Yeah, not for a while though. It'll probably come back fast."

"It had better," Mom said. "You're not done on 'Ten-31' till almost June. Good thing Dmitri is blocking out studio time again." Dmitri owned the studio where Mom taught, where she and Ray trained, and where I'd spent most of my adolescence.

"Are Mike and Paula trying out?" I asked, referring to a couple who had been producing knockout work with the Underground Cabaret for a little over a year. Mom had coached them in Latin technique for a while.

"Yeah," said Ray. "And Vicky and Red, and Lucas. You remember him, right? I mean, I'm sure other people will show up but those are the ones we know of already. Alison's already talking to Mary and Mike about this big group thing she's seeing for the closing number."

I did not say 'sure I remember Lucas.' I pretended I didn't even hear that. "Is there a show title?"

"She's calling it 'The Great Wave.' You know, from the Hokusai print."

"Yeah, I get it." I'd been doing a lot of research on Japanese art and architecture, ever since the tsunami at Fukushima, when I was still in high school. The way that city was obliterated had put me on a 'what if' thing about how to engineer an entire regional re-build. It was a great opportunity for innovation, but of course it was due to a horrible tragedy - the confirmed death toll was up to nearly sixteen thousand people - so the approach was really delicate. One of my instructors was consulting with planners in Japan, and had assigned the class some non-theoretical problems. I wrenched my mind back to the topic at hand. "Is the show in August again?"

"Yeah, will you be in town? You were interviewing for that internship in Iceland, right?"

"Haven't you heard back about that yet?" Mom said, with a disapproving look. She always thought once somebody interviewed me the decision-making process should be concluded. It gave me the warm fuzzies, but it also cracked me up.

"They have a lot of people to talk to. I'm not expecting to hear till right before graduation. Which is annoying," I conceded.

"It doesn't leave you much time to make plans. Whether you end up going or not."

"Well, if I end up going, they'll be making all the arrangements at the other end. All I have to do is show up."

"Anyway," said Ray, laughing, trying to get us back on track, "if you don't go, will you be staying in town?" I nodded. "And if you do go, when do you get back?"

"It's only a six-week program, I'd be back for the show."

"All right then. We gonna see you again before graduation?"

I sighed. "I don't even know. I kind of doubt it. Let's assume not."

"I'll come down to campus sometime and take you out to eat," Mom said. "You look thin."

"Eh," I said. "I'm eating like a horse, if you can believe it. I think the brain waves are burning it all off." Ray laughed again. We circled back to their competition schedule, and I couldn't help it if that brain of mine started running a little subroutine labeled 'why Ray mentioned Lucas,' because it didn't entirely make sense that he would have. Lucas wasn't part of the whole dance family.

Unless something had changed. And I was not, not, *not* going to ask. I had other fish to fry.

Back on campus, I threw myself into the last few weeks of my senior year. Mom did come down and take me out to eat a few times. I established to her satisfaction that I was feeding myself adequately. She still told me to come over any time to raid the fridge, though she had to know I wouldn't because it is no quick trip to get from USC to Century City. If they ever got that train line finished, I could at least study going there and back, but that's a whole 'nother public engineering problem.

Mom also mentioned, right before finals week, when I really shouldn't have been doing anything but cramming but was instead out with her at Morton's eating everything on the menu, that Ray and Lucas were both going to be dancing in the pro show. And again I thought *why is this even coming up*, because it was REALLY FRIGGING DISTRACTING and not for any good reason. I changed the subject to her own dancing, because she'd let slip that she'd told Ray if they won their division three times she would marry him. I knew he'd been after her about that for quite a while. And they'd been just one mark off winning for the second time very recently. So I interrogated her about where they would be competing, and what they were doing with their routines, and generally pelted her with questions until she was laughing, and that was that.

A couple days later, I got word that I'd landed the Iceland thing, and called Mom right away. "I got it," I said without preamble. "Leaving May 26, the program runs May 30 to July 15 and I'm taking another week at the other end to see the country. Dad's actually going to meet me there."

"Oh, that's great," she said, sounding surprised but sincere. "I didn't know if you'd been able to spend much time with him lately."

"Hardly any," I said. "He's coming to graduation."

28

"Well, of course he is." Her tone made me laugh. "He's so proud of you. We both are."

"Thanks, Mom. I'll see you on the day." I'd been planning to ask her to put a lid on the Lucas mentions, but in the moment I couldn't do it. Not without getting into a whole thing about why wouldn't I want to know. If there was something she and Ray wanted me to find out, I'd find out after I got back from Iceland.

And it wasn't like I'd been *pining* for him. I'd dated. Kind of. Or, well, even 'kind of' was an exaggeration. Looking back over the year, trying to pin down the times I'd been out with a guy in a situation that a reasonable person would describe as a 'date,' I had to admit that those were few and far between. I'd been out with classmates here and there, I'd gone to the ballroom club things here and there, I'd FaceTimed Miguel here and there, but aside from that, I mean, who had time?

But what did it matter, anyway. I still had a master's program to get through, and a guy I had met ONE TIME shouldn't be in my head. I had math to put there.

Iceland helped a lot, I have to say. Not what I learned there, but the experience. Mom and I went to Europe once, Dad took me to Montréal once, but this was my first time traveling outside the country on my own. The stuff I was involved with for my internship was mostly to do with geothermal heat pumps, which are a thing you do not see very much in Los Angeles. The staff and the other students there were not all that different – L.A. is a diverse city – but there was a slight flavor of summer camp about it. I mean, we were all a long way from home, except for the people who actually ran the program. There was a lot of bonding in the conference room and the library, not to mention in our tiny, shared apartments.

The person I especially bonded with was a woman, a year older than me and heading into a Ph.D. program in Sweden. The person I slept with was a seismologist from New Zealand. I heard a lot about why he was in Iceland. I gave him some crap about hobbits, to which he bore a slight resemblance. He was smart, funny, and acceptably proficient in the sack. We agreed not to try to make any more of this than it was, had a great time, and parted friends. It was, if not perfect, at least optimal.

It might go without saying that the hobbit and I parted before Dad got to Reykjavík. That last week of sightseeing and bonding – I really did miss Dad, even though I knew the divorce was best for all of us – was great. By the end of it I was ready to go home.

II - Lucas
June 2016

I had a few gigs between December and March, the same kind of things I'd been doing. It was fun being able to answer "Oh yeah I'm shooting a streaming thing starting in March" when people asked what I had coming up. Then there was a hell of a lot of work to do, getting ready for Vegas. Carbon 13 Productions sent me a ton of material. All thirteen scripts, sheet music for the songs we'd be doing, a list of locations and a guide to their soundstage facility, a cast and crew summary so I could walk in knowing who I was working with. That was really nice. There was a tip-off about what sounded like days' worth of choreography, in styles that were going to be a stretch. They had a trainer, a guy who also worked on a showgirl extravaganza on the Strip, but they included a list of local dance studios. I did not think that was put there in case I got bored. I assumed it meant my ass was going to be in all those studios on a regular basis.

There was also a thing about 'we hope you're brushing up your guitar skills,' which I took to mean 'you'd better be brushing up your guitar skills.' As soon as I finished reading through everything – which told me exactly why they wanted that guitar, where they wanted to use it, and how much I'd better be good at it – I went to Guitar Center and picked one out. A high-end acoustic with its face stained black, because I liked its sound but I also liked the way it was going to look when I had my black leather jacket on.

There were a lot of years (not so far behind me) when spending a thousand dollars on something, even a thing for a job, was inconceivable. But after seeing these scripts, it was clear that Raquel either didn't know what my part was all about, or she deliberately didn't tell me.

Maybe she didn't want me to freak out. I was one of five featured actors, all playing roles that anchored separate storylines that would weave together. It really was a soap opera, and I was one of the stars.

The others were all women. One was a real aerialist, playing an aerialist; her name was Kelly Seda. That was Spanish for 'silk' and it had to be a stage name because if she wasn't Thai I never drove through East Hollywood. Then there was a showgirl, played by a former ballet dancer named Stephanie Lawrence; an illusionist's assistant, played by Meredith Townsend; and a musician, played by Nancy Perez. They had her down as playing electric bass, among other things, and she was going to be one of my love interests. They were like me, people who'd done this or that on stage or in front of cameras, but not really known as actors. We were all going to sink or swim together.

It was an unbelievable opportunity. I alternated between being super excited and being positive the whole thing would either never make it on the air, or would be a legendary flop, and I would never work again. All I could do was be as prepared as possible.

The bulletin board at Guitar Center led me to a teacher named Barry Teller. I spent a lot of hours with him. He took me way beyond the three-chord progressions I'd gotten by with in high school. He had a buddy who was a paparazzo, and that guy took some good candid-style photos that we put up on my social media. Raquel sent me a thumbs-up on that.

Then I told Barry I needed to do a thank-you to someone. He helped me put together a little something set to the tune of 'Lovely Rita.' I put it on video, posted it, and got a row of crying-laughing emojis from the background coordinator who started it all.

I was in Vegas for four months on the 'Behind the Strip' shoot, and it was a hell of a lot of fun. The show was full of sex and drugs and drama, like Raquel had predicted. Lots of nudity, too. All of us in the regular cast spent at least an hour in the gym every day, plus most of us had choreography or dance rehearsals almost every day. The show was being done like the 'Chicago' movie, where most of the songs or dance numbers were kind of in characters' heads - except for mine. I'd been given three solos set in 'real life,' and couldn't believe my luck. I had backup dancers, backup singers, full production. It was killer.

We bonded like any cast. Most of us were from outside Las Vegas, and we were mostly staying in hotels. That meant when we had time off, we were roaming not just the Strip but the back streets. We found the karaoke bars, the piano bars, the places to dance. The head writer on the show was a friend of the dance trainer, who was married to a guy who had a Sinatra tribute show. I dropped in on that show more than once, usually with Nancy and Derek, one of the featured musicians. The three of us hit it off on day one, which was like a combination of the lunchroom scene from 'Fame' and the opening scene of 'A Chorus Line.'

At the same time I was having a blast (and getting my ass kicked) being an actor-dancer-singer-guitar player, I was trying to do some prep for a dance concert coming up in Hollywood. I was cast based on a video I submitted, met the director Alison Jarvet for a minute in L.A., and then had to make tracks for Vegas. The show was called 'The Great Wave' and I had no idea what the story was about, or if it even had one. All I had to go on for that audition was the title and the song list. None of the music had lyrics. It sounded like half of the choreography was being done by a trio of black belts, a former gymnast, and a stuntman. The other half was being done by people who'd been in jazz and contemporary companies. I was fully expecting to be beaten to shit doing this show.

In May the director hooked us up with access to a Dropbox with rehearsal videos and production notes. Now there was definitely a story, based on Japanese, Chinese, and Korean folklore. Two princes and their warriors were battling it out. One cohort was all men; the other was all women. The gymnast guy was playing a kitsune, a magical fox who was the ally of the male prince. I couldn't wait to see how it was going to look on stage.

Vegas was a little far from L.A. for me to get back there regularly to work with people, so I knew I was going to be scrambling. I was giving thanks for all those years learning how to pick up dance routines fast. Ray had told me to fit in martial-arts coaching wherever I could. Once in a while that meant losing out on some sleep. Fortunately, I usually had more action than dialogue, and action was easy to remember.

Toward the middle of June Ray called me up and asked when I'd be back. "I'm supposed to be done here in two weeks," I said. "I'm freaking out a little about 'The Great Wave.' How's it coming together over there?"

"Alison wants you here, like, now. Dress rehearsal's set for August seventh. She's got a full troupe but there's some partner work, and there's no extra bodies."

"I know, I'm sorry." I didn't know what to suggest.

"What if me and Mike come out there this weekend? Are you scheduled, or do you have some time free?"

"I'm not scheduled. I have a night shoot Friday, supposed to be done by two ... but between you and me it'll probably be more like four." I smiled when he laughed. Ray knew all about shoots going over. That cop show he was on was kind of notorious. Around the extras pools they'd called it 24-7 instead of 10-31. "After that I'm not on the call sheet again till four o'clock Monday afternoon."

"Okay, perfect. We can be there Saturday by noon. I'll call this guy I know about studio space. I'm ahead of Mike on the martial arts, but he's ahead of me on the other stuff, so between us we should be able to get you up to speed."

"Thanks, Ray, I really appreciate it. I'll take you guys out to dinner."

"Yes you will, brother." Ray was laughing when he disconnected. I felt so relieved, I was almost laughing too. I'd met this Mike guy at the first-look and we'd clicked. It was clear he and Ray were getting along great, from other things Ray had said since I'd been away. The prospect of having the both of them on tap gave me a lot more confidence that I'd be able to work in to the show in the time available.

As I'd predicted, the Friday shoot ran late. I didn't get back to my hotel room till almost five. Went straight to bed, set my alarm for eleven, and crashed hard. By the time I got out of the shower, there was a text from Ray with instructions to meet him and Mike at a studio on the east side of town. *Bring food*, it said. I decided to get with the show, and called up a sushi joint for a giant load of take-out. I got to the studio with my heavy-ass bag of food right on time at twelve-thirty.

"What ya got?" Ray said, meeting me at the door of the rehearsal room. He took the cold six-pack of sparkling water out of my right hand. I waved at Mike, who was at the barre stretching in a way that would have

35

broken me in half. He waved back from the wrong side of his leg.

I thought, I'm gonna get my ass kicked here today, and answered Ray. "All the sushi in Las Vegas," I said, setting the bag down on the floor and shaking out my left hand. "That's some heavy shit, too."

"With all that gym time you've been doing?" He picked up the bag and said, "God damn," and all three of us laughed.

"There's cold packs in there," I said. "I figured we wouldn't want to eat all of it at once, didn't know if there was a refrigerator here."

"Good thinking," said Ray. "Half for breakfast, and half for lunch. Come on, Elasti-man, let's watch some of this blocking while we eat."

Man was I tired at the end of that day. Ray and Mike both looked a little beat too. We worked through all the troupe numbers so I could get a sense of where I needed to be. The big finale number had a lot of synchronized stuff that hadn't been fully finished. I'd have to work on that with everybody else, when I got back.

They'd also been given permission – or maybe it was instructions – to come up with some partner work for a couple of short pieces that Alison wanted to slot in around a solo that Sam, one of the show's stars, was doing. They'd raided an old routine from 'So You Think' called 'Are You The One' that had a lot of fight elements, and we turned it into a trio. The idea was that we three guys could do it after Sam's solo, and three of the women in the cast would do it to different music before the solo. Ray said that re-using choreography had saved all their asses on Alison's tango show 'Gaucho' the year before.

Mike may have looked tired, but he also looked happy. "Paula's going to love that," he said, referring to his wife. "She got to help make the piece that all the women are doing, but it's not a fight."

"She likes to fight?" I said.

He shook his head, smiling. "She likes to dance hard."

None of us wanted to go out to dinner after that hellacious afternoon, so we all went back to my room and Ray pulled up some of the dress-rehearsal video from the tango show on his laptop, so I could see what he meant. Then I ordered up some drinks and some dinner, and we watched the afternoon's practice video while we ate. Mike and Ray did rock-paper-scissors to see who got the second bed and who got the couch (Ray lost). We all took turns in the shower, and by ten o'clock we were down for the count.

Ray and Mike both had to get back to L.A. by the afternoon, so I took them out for breakfast instead of dinner. We all ate like we hadn't seen food in weeks. "Y'all are going to sleep on the plane, for sure," I said, looking at their satisfied faces.

"But you're going back to the studio, right?" Ray said. I nodded, resigned.

Mike said, "Don't forget to stretch," and I just laughed. Compared to his Gumby ass I was like a stick figure made out of Tinker Toys. (Ray was somewhere in between.) It did give me some motivation, though. I mean, I'm a guy; I'm competitive. I set myself a goal to surprise him when I got into the full rehearsals back in L.A.

And I worked on it, I did. By the time the shoot wrapped, I was even pointing my feet. The dance captain for the show noticed, and complimented me. One of the other featured actors had nice things to say about a dialogue scene I'd done. And one of the other singers gave me some props there, too. Even though I had a show to go straight into, I was sorry to leave. For all those reasons, plus the invitations I'd gotten from several women in the cast, all of which I'd rain-checked because … well, because.

I was really sorry after I got home. The apartment was horribly empty, but also kind of haunted. I couldn't imagine staying there. I was going to have to move. For some reason right up to that moment I hadn't thought that. But the more I thought about it, the more I thought, why not move? A two-bedroom had been plenty of space for two people, one of whom had an admittedly crazy schedule, but was way too much for one - especially if I was going to be somewhere else half the time. I mean, I had no expectation that there'd be any more of 'Behind the Strip,' but I'd done enough now to get my SAG card, and that was whole new world territory when it came to auditions.

Anyway, a one-bedroom would be okay, but I probably could get by with a single. Either way I'd be saving a ton of money. So I started thinking about where the most convenient place to have an apartment would actually be, and started looking at what was available, and how much things cost.

I found a building I liked in an area I liked, close to LAX in Westchester, and got myself on the waiting list. Then I went to work with Alison and the others getting ready for the show. Thanks to Mike and Ray I was only a little behind the rest of the troupe.

One day we all met up at this big studio out in Van Nuys and Alison had her experts show us what they'd come up with for the big finale. I had some serious envy going. The number was going to feature wave after wave of movement across the stage, with different dancers doing martial-arts or dance tricks in each wave, in between sections when we all would do these synchronized phrases. Even with just a couple of them at a time doing the moves, it reminded me of the Shaolin-inspired sequence at the beginning of 'Shanghai Noon,' where it looks like a thousand warriors all doing exactly the same thing at exactly the same time. I could imagine how it was going to look on stage: seriously cool.

But the envy came in because the climax of that finale was going to be a relay of a trick called a 540, a huge ballet jump where the dancer launches with his back to the audience, does a full rotation in the air and then whips the trailing leg over for another half turn before landing, facing the audience. There was no way in hell I could learn to do that in the time remaining. I had plenty of jumps, flips, and turns in my bag of tricks, and Alison had already told me to work up my wildest b-boy shit for a solo pass, because I was the only hip-hop person in the cast and she was throwing me a bone, but … yeah. The biggest guy in the show (the stuntman) couldn't do the 540, and Mike's wife couldn't do it; we all hung in the wing area and watched the first time the nine who could throw it did the relay.

It was a knockout. Even though it was a ballet trick, with everyone in their gi-inspired costumes it was going to look like kung fu. Each dancer had a different exit. All of them left the stage, before the princes Sam and Mary returned for a brief duet, still to the finale music, that resolved the adversarial main storyline. They finally bowed to each other, stepped away and then struck a pose.

"That's where you fly," Alison said, stepping back on stage. "We're going to roll out wing curtains, and the

Flyers will be there to hook you two on the cables. We'll push some fog and up you'll go. Good?"

"Brilliant," said Mary. "You right, Sam?"

"Yeah, I like it. It's good to come back to that after our fight in act one." I'd seen the blocking video, so I knew what he meant: they were using flying rigs for their duel number. Even in the gym with the rigs showing, I could tell it was going to kill on stage. I'd heard about those rigs though. I was not sorry that my part didn't call for that.

Then Alison gathered us all together and gave us her notes, including some changes to the rehearsal schedule leading up to dress, and turned us loose. I caught up with Ray and Mike on the way out. "That looked freaking amazing," I said. "Have you always been able to do that?"

Mike said, "I first learned it in high school."

"I had it for a minute toward the end of high school," said Ray. "I was a lot lighter then, though. We've all been working out like maniacs."

"The audience is going to go nuts. Especially when the women do it."

Mike nodded. "Alison really wanted the women. Mary's had it for a long time, she and Alison coached the others."

"It's good nobody mentioned it to me," I said, giving Ray a sidelong glance that said I kind of wished he had. "I probably would have tried it back in Vegas and, like, broken myself in half."

He and Mike both laughed. Mike said, "That's why we didn't mention it. Nobody should try that without a spotter."

"Well, I'll see you next time. Gotta go sign the lease for my new apartment."

"Oh, you're moving?" said Ray.

"Yeah, you know. That two-bedroom was too big. Found a nice single over in Westchester. The building's got a pool area with a gas grill. I'll have you guys over once I get settled in."

"Sounds good, brother."

Mike had moved off, and Ray was about to, but I stopped him by saying, "Hey." He turned back with an inquiring face. "Why did you forward my email to Grace that time?"

He studied me for a second. "I thought there might come a time when you two might want to get in touch. I didn't think I needed to be in the middle of that." I couldn't come up with anything to say. He smiled, almost laughing, and moved along.

It's times like those when you think, damn it, why can't guys *talk*. I truly sucked at it. And I kept tripping over the fact that Grace and I were not a thing. Might never be a thing. At my age, I should not be crushing on someone like I was fourteen. All the happily-partnered people around me did not help. So, as usual, I focused on the work.

III - Grace
August 2016

After I got back from Iceland, I did something unusual and took some time off. I'd moved out of my undergrad apartment in the five minutes between graduation and the trip, so all my crap was back at Mom's house. The plan, at the moment, was for me to live at home for the four semesters of the master's program, though that plan was eligible for revision after I'd been in classes for a while and knew what the commute was really like. At any rate, I'd be back at USC in the middle of the month, and I couldn't really think of any way to use my break productively, so: time off. All of two weeks.

Sometimes, I realized, I was maybe a little too type A for the real world. But I was constitutionally incapable of staying home and, whatever, watching TV for two weeks. The people I considered real friends, the kind I might have wanted to spend time hanging out with, were either working adults or not in Los Angeles. So I ended up, maybe inevitably, taking some lessons. Not in anything related to civil engineering, but in kung fu and salsa.

Ray's friend Danny and his wife Kate, who were both in 'The Great Wave,' were both black belts. Kate managed a dojo in Santa Monica. They also knew a friend of a friend who ran a salsa studio in Santa Monica. Thus, my two-week break was spent largely in Santa Monica. I wasn't expecting to see anybody I knew, since most of the dance people I knew trained in West Hollywood and I didn't even know any kung fu people (except, of course, Danny and Kate).

But, also of course, the last three Sundays of August were the performance dates for 'The Great Wave,' and where better for cast members to run some of their kung fu stuff than under Kate's watchful eye? I don't know why I didn't expect it. It was a surprise when Lucas showed up, coming in with Sam and Mateo. Those guys smiled and waved - I'd known them for a while, since Mom started training them for the Gay Games - then went past me to dump their gear on a bench, but Lucas came over to me.

"Hey Grace," he said, sounding pleased and surprised. "I didn't expect to see you here."

"Hi. Nice to see you again," I said, then added nonsensically, "I've got a couple weeks before classes start again."

"And you just can't take time off, huh." He looked amused, but in a way that said he understood. And I thought probably he did. I had … okay, I admit it, I had Googled him. I had found his website and found out about the arts magnet school and his dance crew and how he'd been barely twenty-one when the crew made it to the final round of ABDC, and how since he stepped out of his crew he'd done so many shows, and background in so many TV episodes and movies. The guy worked. He wouldn't find it strange that I couldn't stop moving. Except guys, so often, really did seem to think it was strange.

I pulled my brain back into the correct lane of traffic and said, "Nope. How's the show coming together? Ray looks a little tired."

He laughed. "We're all tired. I got back from Las Vegas at the end of June and it feels like the only thing I've done aside from work on the show is move to my new apartment."

I was really curious about that - the move, I mean - but it was none of my business so I didn't ask. Instead I asked what he'd been working on in Vegas, so he told me. The thirteen episodes were going to be released in September. I promised to watch. And then Kate came out to get me for our session, and Lucas went over to the other mat to work through some stuff with Sam and Mateo, who'd been kindly pretending to ignore our conversation.

Maybe the past year of practice in compartmentalizing Lucas made it easier for me to concentrate, I don't know. Anyway, it was a good session. By the time Kate turned me loose, I had almost forgotten the guys were even there.

Okay, no, I hadn't. He was even better-looking than I'd remembered. The overtly-Elvis hairstyle that he'd apparently liked enough to keep after the shoot finished was extremely flattering. The sports tank he was wearing showed off a gorgeous set of golden-brown shoulders and arms. The junction of his neck and chest was structurally perfect. It had never really occurred to me how enticing that area could look. He was so fantastically different from every man I'd been around for the past year. It was so completely unfair of the universe to drop him in front of me again.

And then the frigging universe did it AGAIN and I totally wanted to scream. I was at the dance studio for a private salsa lesson, a couple days later, and he came in. His gaze went straight to me and he must have seen the WTF in my expression. He looked a little stricken and said, "I swear I'm not stalking you."

It was such a ridiculous idea that I laughed, and his expression eased, and I shrugged, like what can you do, and went on with my lesson. This time after I was done I hung out and watched what he was doing, which appeared to be a samba lesson. I started to get really curious, because one thing I did know about the upcoming concert was, there was no samba in it. So there I sat, watching like a groupie, and when he was done he came over and sat beside me.

"How was that looking?" he asked. "It's for the show."

"The Vegas thing? Are they doing some more?"

"Yeah, found out yesterday. Thirteen more episodes, shooting starts in October."

"But samba?"

"Well, last time they gave me three solos. I'm still not sure they're all making it to air, but I guess I'll find out soon. Anyway, this time they said my numbers are going to be bigger, and could I knock up some samba for one of them, 'A Little Less Conversation.' You know that song?"

"I love that song. They're right, it's a samba. Is there a ballroom person in the production?"

"They're working with this guy in Vegas with a big studio, big teaching program. He runs the Emerald Ball?"

The Emerald Ball was a huge ballroom competition in Los Angeles; Mom nearly always took students to it. "Oh, that guy! He's great. Well, heck, now I *really* want to see it."

He laughed, and I realized how that had sounded. I started to say something else but he shook his head, like it was okay. "Are you coming to opening night?"

"No, I thought I'd come to the last show. That way I can stay for the after party. And I'll have a couple of weeks of classes under my belt so I'll have some idea whether I'm going to survive."

"You're going to do great," he said. "All I hear from Ray is how smart you are."

"Gaahh," I said, embarrassed. "I'm sorry."

"He's just reminding me there's more to you than beauty," he said, then blushed and turned his head away.

I was speechless for a minute, mind racing. Did that mean he liked me? Did that mean Ray knew he liked me? Did that mean Ray didn't mind, or actually approved? What the actual heck did it all mean? "Um," I said, sounding anything but smart. And since I couldn't think of anything to say, and I couldn't think of anything to do that wasn't 'grab him,' I gathered up my gear and left. Gave him this half-assed wave as I left, still so flustered that I didn't even try to guess whether I'd been completely, unforgivably rude.

By some miracle I didn't run into him again the next few times I was at the dojo or the studio. I took advantage of the lessons to work out some fairly severe frustration, because seeing him again had reminded me that I had not had a boyfriend, or anything like one, for longer than I would have liked. I made up my mind that as a grad student I was going to Make Time for, if not romance, then at least the occasional booty call. The booty calls during my internship had gone a long way to keeping my brain fully functional.

I told myself pretty firmly that I was not, under any circumstances, going to talk to Mom or Ray about Lucas. Lucas was officially none of my business. Which would explain why I caught up with Miguel for an obsession session. His reply to my text was *Chica you need to get laid*

I wrote back immediately, because he was right and what else did I have to do: *Iceland seems like a long time ago and the universe keeps dangling the hottest Mexican in the world in front of me*

LOL is it that Lucas guy? Because of course I told him about Lucas more or less immediately. I must not have answered fast enough because another message rolled in. *Where did you see him?*

Every fricking where. At the dojo. At the dance studio. He's doing a show with Ray and I'm pretty sure he's been at the house too. Thank God I wasn't there, he makes me thirsty

LMFAO Is he still married?

As far as I know. Distract me

I broke up with that guy from Berkeley. It was all politics all the time and IDGAF

LOL you need to care a little more, Latino voters would control if you would all get your asses out there

Half those motherfuckers talk like they're going to vote for that fucking idiot from The Apprentice

Ugh don't tell me that

I always tell them count the number of your friends and family who are hiding from ICE already and then think about who you want running things

Exactly but ugh. You're good right?

I'm great amiga. This school is fantastic, I've got an interview with Lucasfilm in a week

HOLY CRAP MIGUEL why are we wasting time talking about my nonexistent love life?!

LOL it's only an interview. I'll let you know how it goes

Yes please. I'll light a candle and cross my fingers and whatever else. But now I'd better open a book

For sure. TTYL chica, besos

Y abrazos. I disconnected, stared at the pile of textbooks on my table, and sighed.

Mom and I went to closing night together. She'd had the usual last-minute nonsense with one of her students, with whom she was (in my opinion) altogether too easy-going, but I guess the guy was harmless, and anybody who paid for that many hours of instruction without ever getting inappropriate was in the Good Guy column. Anyway, she blew into the house about an hour before showtime, dashed down the upstairs hall cursing under her breath, and was showered, dressed and ready in thirty minutes. I'd been keeping tabs on her progress by listening to the narration, which got funnier and funnier as we got closer to Time We Need To Leave, and called out "I'll go start the car" as I heard her close her closet door.

She was out the front door barely a minute after me. I had the car running, and handed her a travel bottle I'd filled with water. "Thanks," she said. "I love Aaron but God Almighty some days I want to break one of his legs."

I laughed for about the first five minutes of the drive. When I finally sobered up we were well out of Century City. I asked her to tell me more about what she was doing with her student, because I knew that would keep her mind off being late. The shows at Chrome, back before I was old enough to go see them, used to be a rather more casually-organized affair. Sometimes they started as late as ten or ten-thirty. The new regime wanted its members - and its audience - to take the place seriously as a venue for professional theatrical dance, so when a show was posted to start at eight-thirty, it did.

We got lucky with traffic, anyway, and it was only eight-twenty when I turned the car over to the valet at the club. We went downstairs to the performance space, found our reserved table, put in our orders, and had drinks on the table before the lights went down. The night's menu was a sort of pan-Asian tapas deal, which went really well with the Asahi I'd ordered. Mom was drinking Kung Fu Girl Riesling and seemed pretty happy with that, too.

I'll confess, I don't see a lot of dance except on the stage at Chrome, so I don't know if the show would have seemed so great to a completely objective observer. But I kind of don't care; I loved it, and really that's all that matters, isn't it? I loved seeing Sam, one of the sweetest men on planet Earth, so beautifully embodying a warrior prince. I loved seeing Mary as his adversary, a warrior in her own right, leading a group of other tough, powerful women. Mateo was mind-blowing as the kitsune. He morphed not only from human to animal, but from male to female.

I loved the mix of dance and kung fu, too. (There were other styles mixed in, but I wasn't in a position to pick out what was tai chi and what was tae kwon do or whatever, so let's call it all kung fu.) I'd seen plenty of wire-fu movies, and that kind of stunt could look like crap even with movie tech to clean it up. It was much harder to pull off on a live stage. A group called the Kung Fu Flyers put a wire-fu number into an Underground Cabaret show back in 2012. They were wrapped into this show, for obvious reasons. Every time somebody flew up off the stage the audience went OOOHH.

Honestly, I love watching people dance. When Mom first started, I was little, and all I really knew was that she looked pretty and she was happy, and the music was fun, and her dresses were colorful and sparkly. I'd pretty much grown up watching her thrive on it, seeing how her students responded to her, and seeing the incredible open-hearted diversity in the studio where she taught. The owner, Dmitri, created this environment where people could be who they were, and do what they wanted, and as long as everyone was kind to everyone else, it was all okay. That's a great environment for a kid to experience. I hope it exists in other contexts, but I got to know it in the context of dance.

I also got to know how people work when they love something. People who dance - who stick with dance - generally do it because they can't not do it. There's discipline, sure, and ambition; but there's also this almost obsessive love. Even dancers who do it as a sport are still completely besotted with it as an art form. You can tell just by watching, say, a competitive dancer working a move over and over again in front of the mirror. You might think she's watching herself and kind of getting off on it, until you realize her attention is glued to, like, the angle of a foot. She'll repeat and repeat until that angle is perfect. That angle may be completely irrelevant to the technically-correct execution of a move, but completely essential to making a finished line look beautiful. It's like the difference between a drop-in bridge from the Army Corps of Engineers and Calatrava's Sundial bridge in Redding. Both get the job done, but one is art.

Anyway, to recapitulate, I thought it was a great show. I hoped one day I'd help build something that would make people feel the way I felt after that show: energized, interested, inspired. I tried to be objective about it, looking at the table talker with its list of the numbers, the story synopsis, and the cast. Trying not to absolutely drool over Lucas. Because he was great too. He was totally believable as a warrior. There were quite a few taller dancers on that stage – Red Warner was six foot three, Sam and Mike were six foot one, Red's wife Mary was six feet – but Lucas brought a scary-exciting feral quality to his character. When he threw some of his b-boy tricks, he didn't look urban. He looked animal. I looked at the lineup of dancers at the curtain call, applauding and yelling like everyone else in the house, glad I could say 'the show was fantastic' without mentioning anyone specific, because I could have gone on about him for hours. I was going to have to get my own copy of the DVD.

Then I had to hang out, more or less patiently, until the end of regular business hours, when those who weren't on the list for the after-party would be politely invited to leave, and we could finally hug and congratulate our friends and family. And, okay, others.

When the room was cleared and the cast started coming out from backstage, I slid off my bar stool and stood by the table. I wasn't sure who I was there for at the moment. Ray was in the first group to exit, coming over to Mom as if he'd known exactly where she would be.

"You were so good," she said as he got to us. "I love to see you fly like that." He smiled, lifting her down from her barstool, wrapping his arms around her and kissing her. Don't get me wrong. I'm really, truly, honestly happy that Mom and Ray found each other, that they have what they have. But they have set the bar awfully frigging high. I was looking away, because being happy for them doesn't mean I want to watch them snogging, when Mom said, "Lucas will be out in a minute."

I gave her a sideways look that surely said 'why are you telling me that.' She shrugged a little, raising her eyebrows, and Ray laughed. I glared at him. "What?" he said.

"Why do you guys keep telling me things about Lucas? Last I heard, he was not somebody I should be interested in," I said, aggravated beyond tact.

Ray said, "He's a good guy."

Mom leaned a little bit closer to me, looking at something behind me, and murmured, "And he's not married anymore," barely loud enough for me to hear over the music.

I stared at her for a second. Then I knew who she'd been looking at and turned around. Lucas was about three feet away, all his attention on me. Still beyond tact, I said, "Are you not married anymore?" He glanced at Ray, as if for permission to answer, and I caught a nod from Ray in my peripheral vision.

Lucas looked back at me and said, "My divorce was final last month." Under those serious eyebrows and long straight lashes his gaze was cautious but warm.

I felt this swamping rush – a great wave! – of possibility, commended myself for having worn the cute, short dress instead of the blue jeans, and said, "Then let's dance."

III - Lucas
August-September, 2016

It's fair to say that 2016 was a life-changing year so far. The part on 'Behind the Strip' was already getting me noticed, thanks to all the teasers the production company released. I had lots of fresh stuff on my social media, some with cast members from the TV show and some with the dancers in 'The Great Wave.' Getting divorced: well, it was life-changing, if not in a fun way. Sharysse was happier. I couldn't feel bad about that. And I couldn't feel bad about my part in our marriage, from beginning to end. I did my best to be a good husband and to make it work. She was cool about it, too. When a video got out from Las Vegas of me singing on stage with Gino Corsetti, Sharysse sent a note that was half-teasing, half-affectionate. I guess we did something right if we could still be friends.

And now this show was over. The hardest dance job I'd ever done, with the most diverse company of dancers. I learned so much, and we were all friends now too. It's almost impossible to do a stage production and not bond with at least some of your cast mates, but there were actual tears backstage. We were all saying things like 'see you next year' and 'we'll do this again.' If not this exact show, something else where we could all break out our absolute best on a stage where everyone else was great.

Then I went out into the house and all I could see was Grace. It was like she couldn't even be bothered to be polite and say hi, great job (or whatever), because the answer to that one question was more important than anything else.

Julia and Ray both had to work the day after the show closed, so they left after about a half hour. I'd given

Ray a lift to the club, since he knew he'd have a ride home. We exchanged signals that amounted to 'I'll bring her home' before he walked away, shaking his head and smiling. I kept dancing with Grace, not even pretending I was interested in changing partners. Pretty much everyone else in the cast was partnered up anyway. Even Alison's husband (a perpetually overworked project manager) was there, and even he was dancing.

We took a break about half-past midnight and got some Pellegrino at the bar. "So when do you have to be home?" I asked her. "You're back in class now, right?"

"So right," she said, grimacing a little. "I shouldn't stay out too late. Can I ask you something?"

I could guess what she wanted to know. "Anything."

"Why the divorce?"

"My wife - Sharysse - met someone else. One of those times I was out of town." I shrugged, as if it wasn't a big deal, but I'm not sure it came off. Calling her 'my wife' was a bad slip; it said what I hadn't admitted even to myself, which was that I wasn't quite over the breakup. It was one thing to know the relationship had run its course, and to be essentially okay with it; it was another to be completely objective about it.

I could tell from Grace's expression that none of that nuance escaped her. She didn't ask anything else. She said, "I've got basically two more years of school. Once I'm done, I might be moving out of L.A. I have to get three years of experience before I can be licensed. So I might be traveling a lot, regardless."

In other words, she wasn't looking for a long-term relationship. It felt like a punch in the chest, even though I knew I wasn't ready for that anyway. "I have to travel a lot, too," I managed. She nodded. Then I lost my head and added, "But you know how to find me." She smiled.

I hooked a thumb over my shoulder. "Do you want to dance some more?"

She shook her head. "Let's go outside for a minute. I'm going this way." She tipped her head toward the hall where the restrooms were. I watched her walk off, then thought *not a bad idea*, and went the same way. I wasn't sure what was about to happen, but being comfortable going into it seemed like good strategy.

I was back at the bar when Grace returned. She didn't say anything, simply took my left hand in her right and started walking toward the stairs. We went up, went out the exit door, and were halfway across the parking lot before she stopped. She was still holding my hand. Instead of turning toward me, she rolled into my arm, ending with her back tight against my front, her left arm wrapped across her middle. She fit so perfectly against me, my body instantly responded. I said, "Jesus, Grace," but I didn't move away.

"We probably shouldn't start anything," she said after a moment. "The timing sucks. But I can't get you out of my head. I want you to touch me."

I put my free hand on her shoulder and ran it down to her elbow, then across to our joined hands. She tipped her head back and I leaned my cheek against hers. "Where?" I said softly. "How?" I felt like if I kissed her, and then had to take her home, that was going to be the most awkward drive ever. It was so crushing, but so funny, that I smiled.

"Quite a problem, isn't it?" she said, with a laugh in her voice. "I'm not getting in a back seat with you. I can't take you up to my room in Mom's house. And it would be a hundred percent insane for me to go home with you."

"How about this," I said. "I'll take you home to Julia's. We'll get out of the car. I'll try to kiss you. You

55

can slap me or kiss me back. And then I'll go away. Maybe that's as far as this will ever go." I stopped then because I wasn't sure what she was thinking. Her body was so tense against mine, she was almost shivering. There was no way she couldn't tell how turned on I was.

"Or maybe it'll give us something to think about," she said after a moment. "For the next few months." She paused, giving me time to catch up and realize she meant till the end of my next shoot. "What's another few months, anyway." We both laughed a little. Then her fingers loosened around mine and we slowly let go of each other. I stepped back, and waited for her to make eye contact, because I wanted to be sure I'd understood her. When she eventually did, and I was, I started back to the valet stand. The guys there had been busy enough, and the whole encounter had been brief enough, that I don't think they'd really noticed. Grace didn't seem to care anyway.

When the car came around, I opened the passenger door for her, watched her pull her gorgeous legs into the car, and then shut the door. I slid into the driver's seat and looked over at her. "You're so beautiful," I said, before I could stop myself. "Why'd you have to be so smart?" She laughed, long enough that I started to laugh too. I rolled out of the parking lot and started toward Century City.

When I pulled up at Julia's house, there was a light over the front door and a faint light upstairs. "Is that your room?" I asked, putting the car in Park and turning the key. The engine shut off and it seemed very quiet.

"Yeah," she said. "Mom does that, leaves the reading light on. I wasn't sure I'd stay at the house the whole time I'm in grad school, but the commute hasn't been so bad." She turned to look at me, and the space between us seemed suddenly way too much, or not nearly enough. As if she agreed, she opened the door and got out, moving fast.

I thought, *shit*, and got out myself, going around the car. She hadn't moved away, the way I'd thought she meant to. As I closed the distance I lifted a hand and slid it into her hair, now longer, almost halfway down her back. It was as silky-smooth as it looked. I closed my hand lightly over the back of her neck and her eyelids dropped a little. Her lips parted. I thought, *yes,* and kissed her.

Her hands came up, but not to push me away. One of them wrapped around my back and the other went to my chest, then slid under the collar of my shirt and over the skin of my shoulder; her thumb rested in the hollow of my throat. She took her mouth away from mine to say, "This has been killing me ever since you came into the dojo. Your neck is so frigging perfect."

Her hand on my bare skin was about enough to make me forget all my good intentions. I kissed her again. Her other hand came around to my front and she started unbuttoning my shirt. I was still kissing her when she got the shirt open, and both hands on my body, with one stroking up around the back of my neck and into my hair. My other hand went to her body, resting uncertainly on her hip until she pressed close. Then I let it go down, around her sweetly-curving ass, and pulled her tight against me. She murmured something, low in her throat, and moved a foot back. I followed as she took another step, and then we were leaning against the car, her body trapped between mine and the metal, and it was my turn to make a sound. I moved against her as if we were naked. She laughed against my mouth, and spread her legs a little. "Jesus God, Grace," I said, dropping my head to her shoulder. "I can't fuck you up against a car."

"No," she said softly, "but touch me. Lucas," and the sound of my name nearly sent me to my knees, because all at once I realized she hadn't ever said it to me. I didn't need another invitation. I reached down for the hem of her dress and tugged it up, enough to get my hand under it, then up her thigh to her panties, and then underneath those. Now it was her turn to drop her head onto my chest, to sigh and whimper and then before long to gasp, her head going back so I could kiss her while she came.

I wanted more than anything to turn her around, to bend her over the car and sink into her. Instead I took my hand away and let her move that little bit so that her dress fell back into place, moved myself back that little bit so it wouldn't be quite so obvious how badly I wanted to do all that, and other things too. I had a feeling if I had taken her hand and brought it to me, she would have done whatever I needed. But this time, at least - and God I hoped there would be another time - this time was for her. So I gave her some space, tried to settle myself down, and waited for her to go inside. Waited for her to leave me.

She did, of course. But not before saying, "That's definitely worth thinking about," and kissing me again. I don't think I said anything; I can't remember. I know I didn't ask if I could email her. I watched her go, then buttoned up my shirt, got back in the car, rested my head on the steering wheel until I was calm enough to drive, and went home.

There was an email.

> Lucas Gutierrez. I've been saying your name in my head for a long time. I liked it but not as much as I liked what you did tonight. In the show, and after it. FYI this is messing with my

head. I promised myself I would date this year. I'm still going to. You should too. If you write to me I'll answer.

Grace Hart

Thank you, God, I thought. There were a hundred things I wanted to write to her, but all I actually did write was *Tell me about what you're studying.*

I didn't have to go straight back to Las Vegas. I did have to get there in time to rent an apartment before starting rehearsals. I spent the day after 'The Great Wave' closed mostly lounging around at home, doing social media, talking to my agent, and texting Ray. My first message was: *Did Grace say anything?*

He must have been lounging around too. I knew he wasn't called for his show till after the Emmys. *About last night? No. Something happen?*

Not really. I kissed her

I'm guessing since she didn't mention it that she needs to think about it for a while

Would she have mentioned it if she didn't like it?

He didn't bother answering that stupid shit with a text. He called me up. "Brother, you need to get your head straight."

I could hear the smile in his voice. "I know it. Are you sure you and Julia are okay with it if something happens?"

"It's not really my place to be okay with it. I mean, you're both single. She's no dummy. And I trust you."

There is so much that goes unsaid between men sometimes. I wished he would just say he was okay with it. He didn't answer the thing about Julia at all, and he had to know what she thought. I said, "She asked me to write to her."

"Oh! That's good. She emailed Julia almost every day last year, even with everything she had going on." After a pause, "You might not want to expect that."

"Ray, I don't expect anything." I put a little stress on 'expect.' He knew Grace had been on my mind for going on a year. He also knew I hadn't been with anyone but Sharysse for a long time. "We're not in a position to date, or even to get together and talk. If I write and she writes back, maybe we'll get somewhere. She said I should be dating."

"Do you want to?"

Only if it's her, I thought, and said, "We'll see."

He laughed softly, as if he could tell that was bullshit, then changed the subject. By the time we got done talking about his TV show, his competition calendar with Julia, and his full intention of holding her to her promise if they won their division three times, I was pretty well calmed down. Enough to think I could get through the next shoot.

A couple days later I got a long reply to my email. It told me a lot more about Grace than it did about civil engineering. I had to Google a few of the engineering things, but I was pleased that she wrote as if she expected me to understand what she was talking about. At the end of the letter, she added *Tell me about your show*.

So I did. I used her letter as a model, and I won't lie: it was basically like taking a writing class, because nothing I'd ever done had involved a long, technical, written explanation of what it was like to shoot an episodic drama. It took me a week. At the end I wrote *I hope you like it when you see it. Tell me about Iceland.*

That's how it went for a few months. We didn't write 'hi how you doing' and go to some kind of awkward are-we-or-aren't-we relationship thing. We didn't talk about whether we were (or weren't) seeing other people. But we told each other about ourselves, about what was important to us. Our families. Our successes. Our failures. Neither of us asked follow-up questions. I wasn't sure why, but I thought maybe we were saving the follow-up. We were laying a foundation.

Even if something else happened for one of us, and we didn't end up building on this, I knew I'd always think of it as a love affair. I saved all of the emails.

After Grace watched the first thirteen episodes she wrote just one line: *Holy crap Lucas if they don't release 'Love Me Tender' as a video single they are as dumb as a box of rocks*, which made me laugh out loud. I forwarded the message to Raquel, who wrote back *whoever that is, is right*. I don't know what she said or who she said it to or if she even contacted them, but a couple weeks later, at the halfway point of the second shoot, the company did.

I'm not ashamed to say it: I watched that thing like six times in a row. I almost couldn't believe it was me. I mean, I still felt this detachment, or disconnect, when I saw any of my scenes; it was nothing like watching a tape of a dance practice. But this was even weirder than that. It was my face, my voice, my*self* sitting on a stool under a spotlight with one foot on the floor like the director wanted (to show off a long leg, she'd said), but the way it was composed and shot, I couldn't help thinking I looked like a star. How could that be? It seemed like a minute ago that I was asked to do my first-ever filmed dialogue.

When I said as much to Raquel she said, "Lucas, you've been working in the biz for almost fourteen years.

61

This is not overnight success. You show up, you do whatever you're asked to do, you know your stuff, you don't act like an asshole, and let's face it, you've got the looks. Chill the hell out and enjoy it."

So I looked at it one more time, thought about how much work I'd put in, and thought *yeah*. I did look like I belonged there. I sang with one hand holding the mic and the other one on my thigh, looking not out at the audience full of extras, or at the camera, but at Nancy, playing the electric bass that was my only accompaniment. Back at the beginning of the second season, the writers hadn't decided whether to make ours a serious relationship. Since the other three ladies all had big romance storylines, though, they decided to make Nancy's arc about her career. This scene was kind of our goodbye.

That wasn't the only way this season was changing. After the election, the writers swerved hard. Our production team was a seething hotbed of resisters and rage – and honestly, so was the cast. There we were, a gang of marginalized ethnic and gender types playing, basically, ourselves. The nature of the show made it possible to write storylines that hit cultural trigger points. The first few scripts had been heavily edited, but the back half of the season got scrapped and completely rewritten. The whole thing was turning into a thirteen-episode protest march set to song and dance.

It was genuinely thrilling, even though all of us knew the streaming company who'd bought us might dump the whole thing, calling it a failed experiment. We definitely all thought there was no way we'd get a third order. So we were balls to the wall. I hadn't told Grace how it was going, since most of the cast didn't even know, but they were planning to have my character and one other – Derek, a black guy, one of the backup musician characters – shot by police in the last episode. If by some miracle the episodes went to air, it would be a great cliffhanger as to whether either of us survived. And if by some bigger miracle we got another order, there was a whole wide world of topical stories we might explore.

I saw Ray and Julia in December. They came to Las Vegas for a competition, and they won. It was their third win in the division. I didn't hear about it till it was a done deal, but they got married, like Julia promised. I wished I could have been there, but maybe it was a thing they needed to do by themselves. They could have gone back to L.A. to get married with all their family and a lot of friends around. Instead they did it right there in Vegas. Fast, simple, and private. After I got Ray's text, I sent one back with congratulations, and asked how much trouble they were in. Ray's reply was only a line of crying-laughing emojis. But the next day he sent a text that said *I am the happiest man in the world.*

I sent one back saying *I am truly happy for you and Julia. Good job champ.* Then I put away my envy and pinned down a time I could see them before they left the city. After that I got back to learning another whole new script, digging in to January.

So there I was, in the middle of the greatest creative experience of my life, having the most challenging relationship of my life, in a state of constant emotional turmoil and loving pretty much all of it, and then I got an email from Grace.

It was time-stamped at six in the morning and reading it felt like being hit in the face. It was the worst thing I ever read.

Lucas. I can hardly write this. Ray is dead. He was hit by a car outside the studio. I'm so sorry. I know you were friends a long time. Mom is completely destroyed. I don't know what to do. You don't have to do anything. If you have any time off, we're having a memorial this Sunday. God fucking damn it I swore I wouldn't do this I need you can you come?

IV - Grace
February 2017

Lucas got there for the memorial. I didn't ask if the show had given him extra time or if he'd already had it coming. It just meant so much that he was there. He was waiting at Chrome, standing by a rental car, when Mom and Dad and I got out of the town car. Ray's parents, sister, and brother-in-law were right behind us. Lucas greeted them, and after they went inside he thanked me for the email, for letting him know before he found out about it from the news. Then he said something sweet to Mom, and after Dad took her into the club he held me while I cried.

"I can't believe he's gone," I said finally. "He was so young. He was so *there*." It didn't make sense, but Lucas seemed to understand.

"I know," he said. "When I first met him I thought, that guy is going to be a star." He looked so sad. I patted his chest, then dug through my bag for a mirror and checked my face; it wasn't too bad, all things considered. Mom had said it was a good thing she was a makeup expert. She'd been holding it together, mostly, but neither of us had really been able to eat or sleep since the accident. We had agreed that we would both take the sedatives prescribed for us once we got home. For the memorial, Mom had tried leveling out with a Xanax.

Digging for something that wouldn't send us off a cliff, I said, "The video is great. I was watching it one day on campus and this girl caught it over my shoulder and went all Valley Girl about it. Like oh my God it's totally awesome." Lucas smiled a little. "Then I said, I know that guy, he's friends with my stepdad, and she squeed all over me. It was embarrassing." That got a tiny laugh. "We'd better go inside. I have to sit with the family. Thank you, Lucas. Thank you for being here."

"You needed me," he said simply, and held out his hand. I took it, and we went inside. It was beautiful to hear people talking about Ray. It was awful.

Back at the house, I put Mom to bed and then went to sit in the garden room with Lucas. He showed up, out of nowhere, about ten minutes after we got home, while Mom and I were going through the motions of having a cup of tea. "Is this okay?" he asked. I thought, *of course it is*, and stood back to let him in.

Now all of the things we hadn't shared in our emails were hanging between us. The guy I'd been seeing. The girls he might have been seeing. I didn't really want to know. It didn't really matter. We'd both lost a friend. "How long had you known Ray?" I said. "I never asked."

"We met ten years ago, right after ABDC, when we both went out for a dance movie. We both got hired, and we hit it off so we stayed in touch after the shoot. All that time I was traveling. Then when I came back to L.A. we saw each other here and there. Sharysse and I had been married for a while, I was taking acting classes, starting to go out for the special-skills extra calls again. It's crazy how that was right before he got those first couple of big gigs. He threw me a couple of gigs, you know. Things Raquel sent to him first."

"That's how he was."

"Yeah. I'm so glad I got to see him and Julia after they got married." He looked over at me; his eyes were a little bit red. "Do you have to go back to class tomorrow?"

I sighed. "It's the last thing I want to do, but yeah. And I have an internship. Everybody understands a few days off, but any more than that and the only acceptable excuse would be that *I* got hit by a car."

"I have to get back to Las Vegas. We're shooting the last couple of episodes. Grace." He hesitated. There was clearly something he wanted to tell me.

"What?"

"I want to warn you. This season took a turn in the writers' room, after the election. We have a sexual-assault storyline, a deportation storyline, a healthcare-denial storyline. And a police brutality storyline."

I was pretty sure I knew what he was getting at. "Do you get shot, or something?" He nodded. "Thanks for the heads-up."

"There's been some press about the first season, so they're trying to feed it with little teasers, but there's a chance the buyer may dump the show when they see the episodes. They might think it's." He stalled again.

I filled in the blank. "Excessively topical?"

"Yeah. We've still got all the sex and music and dance, but it's not just a soap opera this time around."

I sat back on the couch. "Well, at least they're shooting the whole thing. Any reaction to the video?"

"God, yes. I mean, my family's been nuts, and my Facebook blew up, and the show's social media is on fire. They released a video with one of the aerialists, did you see it?" I shook my head. "You might want to, it's something that wasn't even in the show as a whole piece. The aerialist is this beautiful Thai girl who started out a boy. Her backing track is nothing but violin. It's so different from mine. They're going to release one more, too, a rehearsal video with all the dancers and musicians doing 'My Heart Will Go On.'"

"That's great, that must be such a boost for all the artists. What are your plans? When the shoot is over?"

"Come back to L.A. See what Alison's got in mind for this year's pro show. See whether this girl I like is going to be around." A trace of a smile, soft and hopeful.

"I'm applying for another summer program," I said, and watched the disappointment settle in. "It counts as work experience, like the internship I'm doing this semester. It's in Japan. I'll be here for the show again, though, even if I get it."

"Well, that's something." He gazed at me. I knew he was thinking about a lot of things, from Ray being gone, to me being gone, to him being gone. All I could really think about was how much I wanted to sink into him and let him be my comfort. My shelter. From the planes of his face to the lines of his body to the timbre of his voice, everything about him said *This is the one.* I didn't know if he could see any of that in my face. After a long moment, he asked, "Are you going to be okay?"

"Yeah," I said after another short pause during which I seriously considered throwing myself at him. "I've already got an appointment with a counselor. I'm not going to try to be tough. You shouldn't either."

"I know. I won't."

"How did you cope, when Robert was killed?" That was one of the things I'd learned through our letters. His older brother, who wasn't even in a gang, had been gunned down in a drive-by shooting. His parents had moved even though they couldn't really afford it, leaving the neighborhood with their other three kids.

"Well, that was when I got into the performing-arts school, after we moved. Mom and Dad both had to get new jobs and they were on opposite shifts, so there was always somebody home, but they had to sleep. And I was the big brother now, right? I was busy in school, but I was helping my little sisters. Learning to take care of the laundry and the kitchen and everything."

"So you didn't really have time to just deal." I had wondered. That was one of the follow-up questions I'd wanted to ask, but I never thought it would come up through a situation like this. I didn't even realize I was crying again until I felt his hand on my face, wiping away the tears, before swiping his fingers across his own eyes.

He stood up and held out a hand. I let him pull me up off the couch. He didn't reach for me, but I leaned into him anyway, and felt his arms go around me. "This isn't how I wanted to hold you," he said softly. "Tell Julia I'm sorry."

"I will. I'm sorry too." I stood back a little, and he let me go. We walked together to the front door. I opened it, and he stepped out. "Will you write to me?" He looked back at me with half a smile, then leaned across the distance between us and kissed me. Briefly, but every bit as bewitchingly as I'd remembered. "I guess that's a yes." He touched my face, turned, and walked away.

The email showed up a couple of days later. *Tell me about Japan.*

I don't really know how I got through that semester, aside from those emails. Mom left for Minnesota before the end of February. She hadn't been coping well - or, really, at all. My granddad had been in touch to say Grandma wasn't doing well, so Mom decided to go out to Minneapolis and spend some time there, help her dad figure out the next steps. I would have gone myself if not for school. I was there in that big house alone and feeling a little bit shaky. All of Mom's friends were great, people were checking in constantly. I'd been in touch with my friend Miguel and he called me every week. Mom and I emailed almost every day, I knew more about what was going on with my grandparents than I ever had, and I was somewhat reassured about her state of mind.

But I missed her terribly. Missed the way we used to be, Mom and Ray and me. Daytime, when I was occupied with school stuff, was all right. It was the nights that were horrible.

I realized I'd never been so thoroughly alone. I'd lived alone, technically, for most of my college years; but alone in a busy apartment building was very different from alone in a big house on a quiet street. I didn't like it at all. So maybe it's understandable that I started spending nights with the guy at USC, the guy I'd been seeing off and on through the fall and winter. He said he was in love with me, and I avoided responding because I couldn't say the same but I didn't want to break it off.

Awful, right? I could have called Lucas once he was back in town. I could have said, I'm lonely, come over here. I think the only reason I didn't is that I knew I was leaving again, whether for Japan or for my second-choice summer option, and I was choosing to be unfair to that other guy rather than be unfair to Lucas.

Or myself. Because I had, by now, admitted to myself that when Lucas and I finally took the next step, it might be over a line neither of us would want to cross again.

Mom made arrangements to loan the house to friends of friends for six weeks of the summer, while I would be gone. Getting things ready for that was a helpful distraction. Then I got confirmation that I would be going to Japan, and had more plans to make. Before leaving, I sent another email to Lucas: *Tell me about God.*

I didn't mean the obvious thing. The Underground Cabaret was doing a summer show with the theme 'Cosmic,' and I'd heard through the grapevine that Lucas was dancing in it to a Tori Amos song. I'd see it eventually, of course, on video. But our last two emails had been about nothing more personal than (on his part, in response to my *Tell me about the police*) that the second order of 'Behind the Strip' was going to air and (on my part, in response to his *Tell me about bridges*) some interesting trivia about suspension cable. I had a pretty strong idea why Lucas had chosen that song, but I wanted to know if I was correct.

I didn't get an answer until I'd been in Japan for a week. It wasn't what I'd expected - which would, by this point, have been a well-thought-out and well-composed essay pulling together the grief over Ray and his brother, the lingering pain over his divorce, the conflict inherent in knowing you're on the brink of a new relationship but not being ready, or in position, to step into it, and his gratitude for having the medium of dance to work all that out.

Yeah, I expected a lot. Well, after this much time and this many letters, I knew a lot about this guy. But he still surprised me. The response didn't have any text, only a link to the video of his performance. At first I thought *I could have gotten that by myself*, and felt a little bit like maybe he was blowing me off. Then I watched the video, because of course I wanted to see it anyway, even if only so I'd be fully informed when I sent a reply saying 'if you don't want to write anymore just say so.' That wasn't why he sent the link. I watched it a bunch of times; it said everything he could have written, and reminded me that this, too, was part of who he was. This talent, on top of all the others.

I did what we usually didn't do, and sent a response to the response. *That's great work Lucas. Ray would have loved it.* And then, maybe because I hadn't asked him to tell me anything, he did the same thing, a response to the response. All the reply email said was *I love you*.

71

I didn't write back. Or, more accurately, I didn't send him what I wrote. I knew when he wrote that it wasn't the kind of flippant, casual response a friend might give when you pay them a compliment.

What I wanted to say, I didn't want to put on a screen. I put my head down and powered through the rest of my commitment in Fukushima, then made the long trip home. The second season of 'Behind the Strip' had been released; I sat alone in the empty house and watched the whole thing. Seeing him get shot, even in make-believe, was awful. I was glad he'd warned me.

He had four featured songs this time. The last one was 'Can't Help Falling in Love With You,' because of frigging course it was, in the twelfth episode. He stood on the small stage they'd created for his character, with a couple of backup singers and a pianist. He accompanied himself on the guitar, and though he might have been directed to sing to the camera with that look on his face, it felt like he was singing to me.

I didn't tell Mom about this thing with Lucas. I hadn't told her any of it, and that was unusual. I might have, if not for what happened to Ray. How could I call her up and say, I'm falling in love, when she just lost hers so horribly? I didn't want to talk to any of my Los Angeles friends about it, because they were all her friends too. The word would get back. The only person I dared bring into it was Miguel, and I was desperate, so I sent a text: *Hola amigo did you watch season 1 of Behind the Strip?*

The reply came the next day, which I hoped meant he had time to chat. *Duh yeah had to see the guy you're tripping over*

What did you think?

Ay papi

LMBO TYVM yes exactly. Season 2 is out. I am toast
In love?

Could I lie about that? No, no I couldn't. *Totally*
What does he say?

I haven't told him yet. He told me he loved me. I knew what Miguel would say about that.

He didn't disappoint. *So WTF are you doing talking to me?*

LOL he's doing another show this summer, he's busy. I'm going to closing night, I'll tell him then

Make it good. Tell me what happens

Definitely. Gracias amigo, you're the best

That's what he said

LOL TTYL. He seriously did make me laugh.

IV - Lucas
August 2017

When Grace didn't answer that email my initial reaction was, well, that's it. But I had to send it. I couldn't stand to send one more letter that said nothing important, or one more letter that basically only said what we both already knew. That we wanted to be together. That we weren't ready. Or that we were ready but we were too scared to take the chance.

Or, when it comes right down to it, that I was ready and she wasn't. She had to know, by this time, that when (if) she finally said 'let's go,' I wasn't about to ask 'Where?' If I had been even half right about what she was thinking that day at Julia's house, after the memorial, when she'd stepped into my arms as if she couldn't stand not being there ... then either something major had changed, or it had all gotten too big for a letter.

I wondered if she knew that half of what I'd written since that very first letter was stuff that might never have crossed my mind if it weren't for her. I'd never been asked to *think* that way before. Or, not asked, exactly: challenged.

Though, on second thought, maybe she didn't even realize what a challenge it had been. Maybe she liked me enough that she assumed I had something between my ears. And maybe, I told myself, I should let this play out and quit assuming I was getting rejected. When had she ever made a move that looked like she was pushing me away?

I'd been back in L.A. for months before she went to Japan, and neither of us had done anything about getting together. We kept emailing like we were still hundreds of miles apart. Maybe it was too soon after losing Ray, maybe Grace's workload for school was too much, or maybe both of us were subconsciously looking at all the things that were still in our way and not seeing a way to get past them, or over them, in the time we had.

I had more of my usual work to do, during spring and early summer. Then I had another dance concert. It wasn't the most profitable thing I could have done, and if 'Behind the Strip' didn't get picked up again I might regret blocking out the time for it. But my experience on 'The Great Wave' had been too good to not want to try and recapture it. Even though Ray wouldn't be with us this time. And I hated that, truly hated it.

Alison Jarvet, the director, pinged me in the spring and asked me to collaborate on 'Face the Music.' It was another new approach. The first pro show was a narrative dance concert based on the Beowulf story. Then there was one, the first one Alison directed, that was all tango. After that, 'The Great Wave,' which did well enough with the media that Alison got backing from some private investors for the new show. This one was built around ballroom dance styles, and it had no narrative at all. I was in charge of making four numbers, one for each section, merging urban style with partner dancing. All of us making the choreography and running rehearsals were actually getting paid, at something approaching standard rates. I talked a lot with Raquel, and didn't take any other jobs through September because if Grace came back and said 'let's go' I didn't want to already be halfway out the door again. And if she came back and said 'don't write me again' I didn't want to have to put that in a box while I tried to be creative.

Then the night after dress rehearsal, when I knew she must have been back in town for at least a week and it had taken all my will not to roll up at her house, finally, an email: *Can I see you after the show closes? I'll be at Chrome.*

There was only one possible answer to that: *Of course, see you there.* I wanted to write more. I decided not to, because I really thought if she didn't want to see me, or hear from me, she would say so. She wouldn't ask to see me only to tell me that, right?

So, I went into the performance weeks feeling considerably happier. The show went well and got good initial reviews, which also made me happy, because it was my first time getting a choreography credit since I'd worked with my crew. The last week of the run, I heard from Raquel again.

> Hi Lucas, nothing but good feedback from the 'Strip' team. I guess the buyer was a little surprised by some of the writing choices, serves them right for not checking in earlier, but someone up there must have liked the direction.
>
> But we need to talk about how to make you some more money. How about twenty-six more episodes? With a ten percent raise? If you don't want to, your character dies, and I'll send you a few of these scripts that are piling up. If you do, production starts in October.
> Cheers - Raquel
>
> p.s. Oh yeah also a percentage on a cast album, either way.

I didn't have to think very hard about that one. It was the kind of email every actor wants to get from his agent. I wrote back *Guess I'd better find another apartment in Vegas.* Spent the next week (when I wasn't rehearsing) doing the contract paperwork, organizing my finances, and getting my family up to date. When I showed up for closing night, Mike studied my face and said, "You got good news. About your series?"

I couldn't help smiling. "Yeah, they're picking it up for another twenty-six. I can hardly believe it."

"It's good," he said. "We've already watched the whole thing. Glad to know you're going to survive." A shadow crossed his face; he'd gotten close to Ray too. I did something that guys don't often do, and hugged him. It seemed to be welcome.

"I still owe you," I said when I let him go. "Thanks for all your help last year, and this year. This show wouldn't be what it is without you and Paula. I don't know if Alison's said that."

Even when you know your contribution is important, it's nice to hear it. He looked pleased. "Not in so many words. So will you be moving to Las Vegas?"

"Yeah, pretty much. I'm going to try to keep a toehold in L.A. though." I glanced at my watch and realized we needed to get backstage. "Time to prep, Gumby."

The show may not have had a story but it did have a complex structure, so I didn't have much time to think until the curtain finally came down. I set my phone on the makeup counter while I got changed, which took a while because the whole big cast was back there getting ready for the after-party. I was a little surprised when I heard it ping, because most of the people who'd be calling or texting me were already in the room. When I reached over and got it, I saw a text message from an unknown number. I didn't expect it to be Grace - as far as I knew, she still didn't have this number - but I opened it anyway. And what do you know: *Loved the show! I'm hanging out at the back counter. Brought something for you. OXO Grace*

I texted right back: *Out ASAP got a mob back here XOX*. Then I put on some speed so I actually could get out of there, and wouldn't you know, the way it always happens when you want to GTFO, all of a sudden everybody wanted to talk to me. I had to hope Grace understood, but then I guessed she probably was used to it.

Finally I made my way out of the green room and through the friends-and-family crowd to the back of the downstairs lounge, where she was sitting on a bar stool, wearing a Fifties-style full-skirted dress that showed off her legs and her high-heeled saddle shoes. She'd cut her hair; now it was super short, which somehow made her eyes look huge. I may have had a plan, or at least an idea of something to say, but when she smiled at me all I could do was kiss her.

She laid a hand on the side of my face and kissed me like she meant it. Then she eased back on the stool and looked me over. "You're gorgeous tonight," she said. "This is twice I've seen you at the end of a show. You were gorgeous the first time too. This is for you." She picked something up off the counter and handed it to me. It was a slim leather case. I opened it to see a pair of what looked like house keys, attached to rings on one side. A laminated card was in a pocket on the other side. I slid it out to find a security company's brief instructions on one side, and a code handwritten in Sharpie on the other. I glanced up at Grace; she looked kind of nervous.

"Are these the keys to your house?" It came out sounding a little sharp, because I was so surprised. She blinked.

Then she took a breath and said, "Mi casa es tu casa. I love you," and I kissed her again, the key case still in one hand but the other hand going around her waist. She slid off the stool and pressed close to me, both her arms around my neck.

When we came up for air, two glasses of champagne had materialized beside us. We didn't question it, just picked them up and drank. Then Grace leaned on the counter, smiling at me again, and said, "Tell me about 'Don't be Cruel.'"

"They were going to make it a standalone solo, the director told me. But when the writers started going topical they decided to use it to score the scenes about the healthcare stuff."

"That's what I was guessing. Same deal with 'Trouble' and the assault stuff?"

"Yeah."

"I really love that cover, though. I want to hear the whole thing. Did they ever shoot it all in one piece?"

"I might be able to show you that," I said, leaning in to kiss her again simply because I could. "What did you think of the whole revenge fantasy? Was it too much?"

"No, I thought it was just right. It reminded me of that first Lisbeth Salander movie with Noomi Rapace, did you see it?" I shook my head. "Well, Noomi is, like, *tiny*, right? And that's a plot point. So there's this scene where she's walking in the subway, and a guy starts to go after her, and she totally beats the shit out of him. But she doesn't kill him, even though she clearly could. She's like a cat. She does as much damage as she needs to, to get away. I had a hard time with that movie right up to that point. I thought it said so much about the character."

"So you thought the revenge fantasy said something about Meredith's character? That she wasn't thinking so much of wrecking the guy as of being strong. Building herself up. I should ask her, I'll bet you're right." I drank the rest of my champagne and finally heard the music that was playing. "Do you want to dance?"

She shook her head. "Tell me they're going to release the other two. That edit on 'A Little Less Conversation,' I could see it with the full music-video treatment. Cutting from you singing on stage to you dancing. Tossing the hair off your face like Paul Mercurio in 'Strictly Ballroom.'"

I was laughing. "You've thought about this a little."

"First couple weeks of classes." She shrugged. "Not in too deep yet." She gave me a sideways look, eyes narrowed a bit with amusement. I could tell she was confident about it now. She knew she was going to succeed. It was incredibly sexy.

"Yeah, they're releasing both of them. Big production number on 'Conversation.' Tell me about your schedule this year." I set my empty glass down.

She set hers beside it. "Could we do that at home?"

God, yes, I thought. "Yeah. We could."

"I'll meet you there." She kissed me one more time, and then we walked out of the club to our separate cars. I had so much racing through my mind, it's a good thing I already knew how to get there. I made one stop along the way, for something I thought we might need.

She was standing beside her car, leaning against it, when I got there. I'd taken a few minutes to talk to Alison, to tell her about the new episode order and thank her again for inviting me to collaborate on this concert. I thought there was a chance that giving Grace a few minutes might make her rethink the whole keys thing. I didn't know how long ago she'd had that thought. But I forgot all my doubts when I got out of my car and walked over to her. She lifted her head, gaze on my mouth, and I didn't even stop walking. I held out an arm as I got to her, and she stepped away from the car, letting my arm wrap around her, and walked with me to the door. "Which key?" I said, the case in my hand, and she pointed to the right one. I unlocked the door and we went inside, then I closed the door and flipped the deadbolt. "Grace."

"Lucas."

We stood there in the dark hall, not touching. "I'm going to be doing twenty-six more episodes. We start production in October and won't be done till June. I'm giving up my apartment here."

"That's fine," she said. "You can live here when you're in town." She moved away, and I followed her into the kitchen, thinking about the big, big difference between 'stay here' and 'live here.' She opened the refrigerator and took out a bottle of prosecco, handing it to me. She watched as I peeled away the foil and got the wire cage off, then took a dish towel off the counter and held it over the cork, twisting gently to release it. "You do that like you've had some practice."

"There's a little drinking every time we wrap an episode," I said, smiling. She set two glasses on the counter and I poured the wine. "Anything to eat around here?"

"Always. Mom trained me, you know." She opened the refrigerator again. "What looks good?"

I hadn't eaten since a little after noon, so the answer was 'everything.' Grace took her shoes off and hitched herself up on the counter, sipping prosecco and watching while I ate. After a while she said, "I'm doing another internship with Mr. Weiss. Graduation is in May. I already have a job offer."

"Where?"

"Here in town. I haven't decided yet if I'm going to take it. What do you think?"

I glanced over at her from the sink, where I was rinsing my plate. "You could have ten more offers by the end of the year. Unless it's the perfect job, I'd wait."

"Was 'Behind the Strip' the perfect job?"

"If Las Vegas was a two hour drive from L.A., it would be perfect." She laughed. I dried my hands and turned back to her. "It was the right job, I think. At the right time. It's already opened a lot of doors." She looked so pretty I was distracted. "Where did you get that dress?"

"It's one of Mom's. She left a lot of stuff here. She's not coming back." Grace turned her head a little, so I couldn't see her eyes.

"Ah, damn it. I'm sorry." I went over to her, set my hands lightly on her shoulders, and then got distracted again because her arms were bare and smooth, the dress was low-cut, and I'd wanted her for so long. She didn't say anything, but she leaned toward me and pressed her face against mine. For a moment we stayed like that, then she kissed the side of my neck. I felt it all the way to my toes.

"Lucas," she whispered against my skin, "can we please go upstairs?"

"What's upstairs?"

"A big empty bed."

"Grace," I said into her hair, "can we please go upstairs?" She laughed. Then she slid down, off the counter, against my body because I didn't move back to make space. And when she was steady on her feet I still didn't move back, I leaned against her so she could feel how turned on I already was. I thought for a few minutes we wouldn't make it upstairs because she set her hands on the sides of my neck and kissed me as if I was the only thing in the world that she needed. "I love you," I said when I got the chance.

"I love you too," she said.

V - Grace
August 2017

I hadn't slept in the big bed before. The master suite had been kind of off-limits in my head, even after Mom told me to go through Ray's things (what was left after his parents and his sister came by) and take them to Goodwill. That task was beyond her, and even I didn't attempt it till right before I left for Japan. I completely changed the bedding after she called to talk about the new job offer she was considering, from a theater-arts school in Minneapolis. Much as I wished she'd come back, it seemed clear to me that she was going to do better there than here. Telling her so was probably the most grown-up thing I'd done to date. I went to dinner with Dad to tell him about the Japan experience, and he asked if I wanted to stay in the house at all. It was in Mom's name now, that was part of the divorce settlement, but I think Dad thought she might sell it. She decided it made more sense to keep it, since I might be in L.A. for a long time, or forever.

Anyway, the suite had been functionally vacant for six months and there were no ghosts there. I'd chosen everything in there except the actual furniture. Even Mom's clothes, the things she hadn't wanted to take to Minnesota, were now down the hall in the used-to-be-a-bedroom that had been her business office. So when Lucas and I walked in, I was able to think of the space as mine. Without looking at him I said, "What do you think of the room?"

"Well, it's about as big as my whole apartment. Aside from that I can't seem to really notice anything right now."

I laughed. "I'm going to brush my teeth. Would you like to help me take this dress off first?"

"Yes I would." He stepped close and laid a hand on my back. "Hmm." The zipper was on the side. He found it, and slowly drew it down. Standing behind me, he gathered the skirt into his hands. I raised my arms so he could pull the dress over my head, felt it fly across the room to the chair in the corner, and almost laughed. Then he set his hands on my body, on the silk slip I was wearing. "I've never seen something like this before in real life. Is it vintage?"

"Yeah, Mom found it somewhere."

"You look like a movie star. Like a poster I saw once. What's that one with Elizabeth Taylor?"

"'Cat on a Hot Tin Roof'?"

"That's the one." His hands were still on me, running lightly over the silk, up to my breasts. He let out a breath and dipped his head to kiss my neck. I thought for a second I was going to faint. Reminded myself to breathe. "If you really want to brush your teeth you'd better make a move now," he said, very low, with a smile in his voice.

I stepped away. It took enormous effort. Without turning to look at him I said, "There's stuff in the hall bathroom you can use," and moved a little farther. At the door to the bathroom I finally turned my head. He was watching me, still as a panther and handsome as a stallion. *Speaking of looking like a movie star*, I thought, swallowing hard. There was a lamp in the corner, by that chair where my dress had landed. The light fell across his face at an angle. "God Almighty, Lucas," I said, "if you're not on the big screen within the next couple of years I'm going to demand an explanation." He laughed, his body relaxing as he started to move. I stepped into the bathroom and closed the door.

When I went back out he was standing there again, with his shirt and shoes off. I'd seen plenty of him by now, of course – most of the main characters on 'Strip' showed lots of skin – but boy was it different having all of that in the actual room with me, instead of on screen. I could feel an aura of heat and energy as I walked all the way around him. Neither of us said anything. Then I touched the back of his arm, where his Quetzalcoatl tattoo started, and let my fingers skim across and down, all the way to where the curling, scaly tail feathers disappeared under the waistband of his jeans.

His head went back and his eyes closed, and I slid my hands around his chest. He gripped my wrists for a second. "You'd better take that thing off," he said, his voice a little rough. "I don't want to rip it."

I felt myself go wet. "One of these days I'll wear something disposable so you can tear it off me." He let go of my hands and I wasted no time getting the slip off. He turned around and watched, unbuttoning his jeans and shucking them off. He didn't have anything on underneath. Neither did I. He stepped close again and wrapped an arm around my back, got his other hand under my thigh, and picked me up. I wrapped my legs around him, clung on to his shoulders, and kissed him. He took the few steps over to the bed and then I was on my back, and he was braced over me, and I said, "I'm on the Pill."

"Let's be safe," he said breathlessly. "I haven't been with anybody but Sharysse for a long time, but she had that other guy." He stretched over to the nightstand and got the condom he must have put there. I helped him put it on, mostly because I really wanted to touch him. Then his hand went between my legs and I raised my knees around him, and a few seconds later he was inside me.

"Oh God, Lucas," I said faintly.

"You okay?" he said against my neck, moving slowly. I had one hand clutched in his hair and the other on his thigh, pulling him hard into me.

"Kiss me." He did, and just that fast I went over. When I focused again, he was still hard inside me and I could tell I wasn't done. Maybe he could too. I moved my hand to his hip and gave it a little shove. He rolled onto his back and I went with him, and suddenly he was even deeper. "Holy *fuck*," I said, and he laughed, and we both lost our minds.

I don't know how much later it was when I finally moved again. I think I might have slept a little. When I opened my eyes and turned my head, I saw Lucas asleep beside me. Now that I wasn't distracted by how much I wanted him - though I already wanted him again - I could see that he was fatigued. Well, I knew how much work those shows were. *I'll let him rest*, I thought, grinning to myself.

I lay there for a while, studying him, thinking about what he'd said. He'd been in Vegas, surrounded by all those amazing-looking women, and for the better part of two years he hadn't acted on any of the invitations he must have had? Seriously, I couldn't imagine that every unattached straight female anywhere near him wouldn't have tried for him.

If I'd known, would I have tried to go it alone? I wasn't sure. I hadn't really been in a good head space for solitude, or celibacy. Plus, he had about eight years on me. I wasn't going to ask about his history, because it really didn't matter, but I had to assume that before he got married there had been plenty of women. On the whole, I decided, my calculated foray into amatory distraction had probably been the best course. Because if I hadn't done that, I would have spent the entire time fantasizing about Lucas, and then if we hadn't gotten here, getting over it would have been even harder.

Of course, now that we *had* gotten here, and I knew for sure that what I'd suspected was in fact the truth (that is, that there was nothing about him I didn't like), getting over it would be pretty much impossible. Which made me flash back to Mom and Ray. I'd never been surprised about their bond, because he was great and so was she, but I understood it better now.

My gaze went back to Lucas' face. He was awake, those long-lashed eyes focused on mine, dark and serious. "If you don't want to marry me, you better say so now," he said softly. I smiled, almost laughing. He smiled too. "After you finish your degree. After my shoot. Deal?"

"Even if I get a job in New Zealand?"

"I don't care if you get a job in Antarctica."

I did laugh then. "Deal." I gazed at him for another long minute. "Just so you know, I won't take a job in Antarctica. Or New Zealand." He smiled. "But we can go there if you want. New Zealand, anyway," I amended, because I honestly didn't have much interest in Antarctica.

"For our honeymoon?"

The word made it really real: he was serious. To be sure, I said, "Are you serious?"

He sat up, so I did too. We shifted around to face each other. He took my hands in his. "Grace, I love you. You know there are no guarantees. We both do. But if we get to June and still feel like this, will you marry me?"

I studied him again, thinking of all that could happen in those intervening months, and the compromises our careers would surely demand, and couldn't imagine saying no. Even if I only had him for a few years, even if life was as cruel to me as it had been to Mom, I wanted those years. "Yes, I will. I love you." He leaned close and kissed me.

"You have class tomorrow, don't you," he said, moving his mouth to my throat. "Today."

"Not till two," I said, and pulled him with me as I lay back.

We got out of bed for real about nine o'clock, not too late under the circumstances. The first thing I did after setting up the coffeemaker was find my phone so I could send a text to Mom. Lucas was leaning against the kitchen counter, unshaven and scruffy and completely appealing, watching me. I told him, "If she's free she's going to call me immediately." He laughed. I sent the text: *Hi Mom. FYI Lucas proposed to me last night and I accepted. Love you*

Apparently she was free. The phone rang almost before I could set it down. "Hi Mom. Yes. We've been emailing for a year now. Yes, I went to the show last night. It was great. I met him there, yeah. Well, I gave him keys to the house and then we came back here and, you know." I laughed. Lucas was smiling. "Yeah. His show is going for twenty-six more episodes so he'll be mostly in Vegas for eight months. Uh-huh. Once he's back we'll figure out the next step. Yeah, I'll be in touch. I promise we won't actually get married without you. She wants to talk to you," I said, handing the phone to Lucas.

He listened for a minute, still smiling. "Thanks, Julia. Yeah, I'm really happy. I love her a lot. Yeah, I know. You take care." He handed the phone back to me.

"So Mom? Lucas has to call his mother now. We'll be in touch. I love you too. Say hi to the grands for me." I disconnected. "What did she say that made you say yeah I know?"

"She said Ray would have been so pleased." There was a sheen of tears in his eyes. "You think so?"

I had to wipe my own eyes. "Yeah. He liked you a lot. Call your mother."

"Yes boss." He got his phone out and dialed the number. I could hear it ring a couple of times, then a female voice saying 'Lucas? What's the matter?' and I laughed under my breath while he started talking, because that totally fit what he'd told me about his mother, that she automatically assumed he was in some kind of trouble. I tuned in again to listen. "Yes, mama, everything really is fine. You remember that girl I told you about. Yeah, the one I was singing to." He glanced over at me, smiling. "I asked her to marry me. Well, yeah, she said yes, don't sound so surprised." He rolled his eyes and I laughed again. "I'm leaving for Las Vegas again in a few weeks but I'll bring her to meet you before I go, okay? What? Dad said what?" He laughed. "Most likely next summer. I won't be done with this shoot till June and she's in graduate school. Yeah, you know mama, she doesn't seem to mind. I've got to go now or she'll be late for class. Te amo Mama." He disconnected and looked over at me.

After thinking *yeah, there's no way I could say no to that*, I said, "What don't I mind?"

"That I didn't go to college."

"I really couldn't care less. What did your Dad say?"

"It was mean. He said he never liked Sharysse anyway."

"Jeez, that *was* mean. What did she ever do to him?"

"Nothing, it's because he thought I settled down too soon. Too young." He was standing on the other side of the kitchen and I suddenly thought that was awfully far away.

I moved across the room and fit myself under his arm, body against his, a thought occurring to me. My own certainty might be suspect to someone with that much more life experience. "Do you think I'm too young?"

"No," he said, gazing at me. "You're twenty-three plus two hundred IQ points, or whatever it is. You think things through a little better than I did."

"I hate to break it to you," I said, "but even a genius can be an idiot sometimes. Now let's eat, so I can take you to bed again and still get to class on time." He laughed, pulled me tight against him, and kissed me.

If I could have ordered up a perfect month, it would have been that one. There wasn't a single thing I needed to do except talk with Raquel, listen to a lot of Elvis, and move out of my apartment. I hauled my stuff up to Grace's house and gave notice on my place in Westchester. When she was home we did what you'd expect. While she was down at USC, I worked on prep for the upcoming eight-month shoot. According to the production material I'd already received, I would get a three-week break starting in December, and two weeks around the end of March. That was if all went to schedule. With two seasons behind us, I was fairly confident this next shoot would go smoothly.

Midway through the month, I took Grace out to East L.A. to visit my parents. My sisters both lived elsewhere now, but when they found out about the visit they both made it into town. "Marisol is married, no children yet, her husband Andre is a mechanic at a Lexus dealership," I told Grace on the way. "Viviana is sort of living with a surgical specialist at Shriners in Pasadena."

"What does 'sort of living with' mean?"

"Vivi says they're almost never both awake and in the house at the same time."

She laughed. "Okay, and Marisol is an optician and Viviana is a teacher. Your mom Luisa is a nurse and your dad Cesar works for the Metro. Got it. What do they know about me?"

"Everything," I said. She squeaked a little and it was my turn to laugh. "They know when I met you, how I met you, all about Ray and Julia, all about the shows at Chrome. They know you're studying civil engineering, and you're about ten times smarter than me, and you can dance. They know I was already in love with you a year ago, and Mama is convinced I was singing to you in 'Love Me Tender.'"

"I'm not ten times smarter than you. Were you?"

"Singing to you? Honestly? No, not that time. Not quite. I wanted to, but I didn't know if you wanted that. So I guess I was acting." I sounded surprised, even to myself, and she laughed again. "I was singing to you the last time, though. On 'Can't Help Falling.' Could you tell?"

"Yeah, I could tell," she said. "That was when I decided to give you the keys."

"You ever going to let me read what you wrote after I told you I loved you?"

"I'll show you at Christmas."

I knew I'd have to settle for that. "You want me to come to L.A. on my break, or could you come to Las Vegas when yours starts? There was something I was thinking of asking for, from the show."

"I guess I could go to Las Vegas. What's your idea?"

"They told me to pick a few songs myself this time. I have a list. There's one I want to do for the episode we'll be shooting right before the break. I thought maybe you'd like to be there for the taping. Maybe even my folks and Julia could come." I was driving, so I could only glance over to see her face, but she looked interested. "Did you ever go see Ray work?"

"No, I never did. Mom did a couple of times, she told me about it. She told me it was still like when she was acting, it took all day to shoot a few minutes' worth of stuff." I could tell she was staring at me. "This isn't some scheme to set up a Vegas wedding like Mom and Ray did, is it?"

I laughed. "No, it really isn't. I did that already." I had learned, pretty quickly, that Grace didn't have any issues with my first marriage. That I'd been married, that I was divorced, that I still talked to Sharysse from time to time - none of it seemed to faze her. Maybe because of what had happened with her parents. Or maybe she thought the past was the past. Whatever it was, I appreciated it.

We had a nice visit with my family. Vivi gave me some crap for a minute, in the kitchen when no one else was around, about how I fell for a black girl and then a white girl, and what was wrong with a Mexican girl? I pointed out that her surgeon was Korean, and she just laughed.

It was late when we headed back to West L.A. Grace was quiet. I asked her if everything was all right, and she put her hand on my leg and said, "Of course. I was mostly thinking how nice it was that your parents are still good together after, what, thirty-six years?"

"Yeah, thirty-six. Well, thirty-eight if you count the years they knew each other before they got married. It's a lot, huh?"

"It sure is. If we're together thirty-eight years from now I'll be sixty-one. You'll be sixty-nine!"

"That ain't nothing," I said, smiling. "I'm shooting for fifty-eight. But I'm counting from last year."

"Yeah, we should." She left her hand on me all the way home, starting to stroke up and down my thigh after I turned off the 10 freeway. By the time I parked the car I was laughing, and hopelessly turned on.

"You better be glad there's a gear shift in the way or I'd be on you right now," I said once the engine was off. She laughed, getting out of the car and backing toward the front door. I was only a second behind her, and she kept her back to the door so that when I reached in with the key I was right up against her. I was kissing her as the door opened, and pulled her in with me. Then my back was against the closed door and she was unbuttoning my shirt. We didn't make it upstairs. We barely made it to the couch downstairs.

I really hated to leave L.A. that time. Grace wasn't very happy about it either. She tried to be cool, because obviously we both had these commitments. It was kind of a giveaway when I kissed her goodbye, and she didn't let go. "Hey," I said. "What's wrong?"

"Nothing," she said unconvincingly. "Call me when you get in."

"Well, okay, but Grace." I studied her face. "Can we still email?"

"Oh God yes," she said, looking relieved. "That's what I wanted. Why didn't I know that's what I wanted?"

"You were too busy wanting me," I said, kissing her when she laughed. "Be safe. I love you."

"I love you, too. Go be a star."

The first thing I did when I got to Las Vegas was send her a text to let her know. The second thing was to send an email: *Tell me about New Zealand.*

When I reported in to work, I asked about having the family in for a taping, and told them the song I wanted to do. Well, I gave them the whole list, but I wanted to get in with the request. The head writer, Kathy Donovan, was also the show runner. The whole concept for 'Behind the Strip' was based on a series of behind-the-scenes interviews she did a few years back, published first in a local Las Vegas paper and then by USA Today. Kathy told me, the year before when she was in L.A. for some lawyer business, that she'd never written fiction (much less a TV script) before Carbon 13 approached her about acquiring the material. It was her friends in Vegas who told her to try writing it herself. Obviously that worked out for all of us. She was the person who coordinated with the directors, so I talked to her as soon as I could. "Why this song?" she said. "It's not very well known. I've never even heard it myself."

"I know," I said. "That's why. I had a rental car that had Sirius XM, and put it on the Elvis Radio channel, and it came up. I thought it sounded like the perfect wedding song."

"Um," she said, "this episode doesn't have a wedding in it." She was giving me this look like I'd lost my grip, or maybe I was trying to get more air time. I didn't have much presence in the episode under discussion.

I laughed. "Yeah, Kathy, I know it doesn't. But my life's gonna have a wedding in it pretty soon, if I've got anything to say about it."

"So how do we use it in the episode," she said, and she wasn't asking me. I could see the wheels starting to turn. "I'll take it to the team and we'll let you know." Then she looked at me again. "You have an idea, don't you? Tell me."

"Right now?"

"Lucas."

"Right, yeah. Okay." So I opened my copy of the script for that episode, took a deep breath, and started going through it. By the time I got out of that meeting, I felt like I'd just done three solid hours in the gym. I'd been planning to go look for an apartment, but I was too wrung out. I went back to my hotel, went to the bar, ordered some food and a drink, and sat there alone in a booth, thinking *I can't believe she listened to all of that.* I couldn't have told you whether Kathy would really take my ideas to the rest of the writing team, or if she'd been humoring me. I didn't know why she would bother. Either way, I realized, I felt good about it. And if they did go with it, then maybe I'd be able to take them other ideas as we went along.

Grace's last email had been short, a sign of her demanding classes. She ended it with *Tell me about hip-hop*, which amazingly is something we hadn't covered before. So I took my time writing her an answer, and by the time I was ready to send it I had two pieces of news for her. I added them to the end of the letter, as we'd started to do.

> Found a decent apartment, finally. Not too big, not too far away, some of the other cast members live in the same complex, which is cool. And the thing I told you about in L.A. is a go. I talked to the head writer and we're going to be doing this song I picked, December 15-16, and they say I can have guests. So let's start rounding up our people. I love you so much. I miss you. Tell me about tunnels.

I got an atypical reply the next day, by text: *Not being with you is so much worse now that I know what being with you is like. I miss you. I love you. Can't wait to see you in December. Mom is on board btw. I promise to send you something rational about tunnels sometime soon. Did you see the thing on Pop Quiz about the show?* I was missing her so much at this point that the blatant invitation to have a normal, simple e-conversation was irresistible, so I went looking for the 'Behind the Strip' piece on the entertainment site, then wrote right back: *I've seen it now. That's good stuff. Mama and Dad are def coming in December. Hope I don't screw up*

LOL as if

Please don't ever ask me to tell you about all my screw-ups, I don't want to scare you off

Impossible. Till I get that tunnel thing finished, tell me about all your screw-ups

No way am I putting that in writing. I'll tell you when I see you in person. Classes okay? How many job offers do you have so far?

Classes are @%$&#! Three job offers. None in Antarctica

Glad to hear it. Get some sleep. Dream of me. I love you

I'm going to dream of dancing naked with you on the beach. I love you

She had to write that. *Great now I'm going to be horny all night*

LOL mission accomplished

Grace was right: now that I knew what it was like to be together, being alone really sucked. I went out with various friends from the cast pretty often, to meals or to movies or the dojo or the gym, and made sure everyone knew I had a fiancée. I still got flirted with a lot, but we all knew it was only for fun. I was careful to keep some physical distance whenever I was out in public with one of the women in the cast. Grace had shown no sign of being jealous, but I felt like it would be disrespectful to act as though other people's impressions didn't matter. The show was starting to get some buzz, and the last thing I wanted was for the gossip press to start their bullshit about me. Sometimes you just can't help it, unfortunately.

I was out with Meredith, Derek, and Kelly – the actress who'd carried the assault storyline, the guy who'd been with me in the police-shooting episode, and the Thai aerialist – one night in late November, out to blow off some steam after a couple of tense days. The episode we were working on had a subplot about a gun show, which had been taped in part at a real gun show, and all of us had personal-history reasons to be nervous around guns. Even if they're supposed to be unloaded. Anyway, by the time we got done we were all a little bit high with relief, but still a little freaked out, so we were more physical with each other than usual. Standing closer, more half-hugs or casual touches, that kind of thing. Nothing most people would consider out of bounds, especially not performers. We stayed out until we all felt settled down and ready for the next day's shoot.

I was driving; Las Vegas is not a place where you want to try to rendezvous with multiple cars. At the end of the evening, I dropped Kelly off at her building, then took Derek back to the house he shared with three other guys, all musicians or actors. Meredith lived in the same complex as me. As I pulled away from Derek's place, her phone buzzed. She picked up the call. "Hello? Who is this? John, God damn it, I told you not to call me. Quit changing phones. You're acting like a creep. Stop it." She disconnected, and did a block-caller operation, and said, "My ex."

"How long has that been going on? If you don't mind my asking."

She sighed. "I broke up with him a year ago. He's changed phones like four times. I guess I'm going to have to get a new number."

"Is he stalking you?"

"I don't think so." Her voice was troubled, though.

"Does the show know? They could get you some extra security."

"I didn't want to call attention to it. It's embarrassing. Especially when we had that storyline running, I didn't want to be a victim in real life."

"Jesus, Meredith. Did he do *that*?"

She took a second too long to answer. "Not exactly."

"You have to tell someone." We were back at our complex. I pulled up to the gate, rolled down my window, and waved my access card. The gate opened and I drove in, as usual, and then slammed on the brakes because a guy had walked right in front of the car with a pistol leveled at the windshield. "Fuck!"

"Oh my God," Meredith whispered. "That's him. Oh my God." She fumbled for her phone and pressed 911 and hit Talk. I heard it start to ring, but I was watching as this psycho started to come around the car, pointing the gun at my face. I hit the window button. It wouldn't stop a bullet, but at least he couldn't reach inside. As he stepped to the side I stomped on the gas and zoomed forward, putting out a hand to pull Meredith down, and ducking my head because something told me he would shoot after us, and he did.

I wasn't sure what to do - heading to my parking space seemed like a really bad idea - so I drove around the loop of driveway, trying to see everything, jumpy as hell, while Meredith talked to the 911 responder. She was keeping her head better than I was, I think. All of the parking was completely exposed, so I didn't want to stop. I managed not to run into anything, but I hit the speed bumps pretty hard, mentally apologizing to my car, praying the psycho would come to his senses and leave, because in a minute we'd be back where we started. I slowed on the approach to the gate, wanting to get as good a look as possible at the area (and also there was a kind of extreme speed bump near the exit). I couldn't see him.

"I don't see him," said Meredith. I didn't know if she was talking to me or to the 911 people. Then she added, "Yes, I still want someone to come! This asshole just shot at us! This is where we *live*!" I had my foot off the gas now, rolling slowly toward the gate, and when I glanced over at her she was looking back at me like 'can you fucking believe this,' and I shook my head. "Should we come to the police station? No I *don't* want to go to my apartment, he *knows where I live*, what the fuck?!"

I couldn't believe it either. They wanted her to go home? He could be in there right now. It was nuts. I didn't wait for them to come up with a solution. I knew where the police station was, because we'd taped there several times, so I rolled on up to the gate and waited - nervously, I won't lie - for it to open. Nothing happened except that the gate opened. We left, and went to put in an official report with the cops.

They dug two bullets out of my car. One had come through the driver's side rear window and lodged in the door on the other side. The other had come through the rear windshield and gone into the dashboard. They did the full CSI thing on the car, but they didn't make me leave it as evidence. We didn't return to the apartment complex that night. We stayed in a hotel, in a room with two double beds, and barely slept. Around six o'clock I sent Grace a text, because I wasn't sure if this was the kind of story that would get to L.A. but I didn't want to take the chance.

Hey Grace. Little excitement around here last night. Remember Meredith, the actress from the 'Trouble' storyline? She lives in the same complex as me. Her psycho ex-boyfriend found her last night and shot up my car, we'd been out with some friends from the cast. We're both okay but we stayed in a hotel last night. Wanted you to know in case the news says something different. I love you

At seven, around the time we rolled in to the soundstage where we were taping that day, a reply came in: *Holy @%&$# Lucas! You sure you're okay? I'm shaking just thinking about it. I love you*

Yeah a little freaked out but okay. We're at the soundstage now, lots of security, and the show is sending someone with us tonight. I'll keep you posted, maybe they'll catch this guy fast

Hope so. Take care of Meredith. Take care of yourself. I love you

I love you too

Wardrobe found me and Meredith some fresh clothes, and we went our separate ways. The soundstage had four different sets and on this day, two of them were active. All I wanted to do, really, was get to work so I could stop thinking about anything besides work. It was a slow day, though, and I never did get calmed down.

Eventually my day was over. I've never been so reluctant to leave a workplace. When Meredith finally got done she found me. "They said they're sending two of the security guys in a follow car. I haven't heard anything from the police, have you?"

"Nope. I guess this shit happens all the time."

She giggled, a little hysterically, and we went out. Nothing scary happened on the way to the apartment complex, and nothing scary happened at the gate. The security guys said they would cruise around for a while and wait for us to report back with what we all hoped would be an all-clear. I parked in my assigned space and we both looked around. Neither of us could see anything wrong, so we got out of the car. "I'll walk you to your place," I said, and we headed that way.

The news report had my heart rate up to some kind of danger zone, and it really didn't help to know that Lucas was all right (or at least to accept what the newscaster said about him being all right, because I wasn't going to know it until I talked to him myself) when all I could think of was that he so nearly *wasn't*.

The security camera footage was terrifying. It showed him and Meredith, in grainy black and white, approaching the access door. Then her ex, the stalker, the frigging psycho who should have been drowned at birth, lunged forward into the picture. He came from behind them, grabbing for Meredith with his left hand and pointing a pistol at Lucas with his right.

What happened next, exactly, was hard to decipher because of the speed. I'd ask Lucas to explain it to me when I finally got through to him. After two voicemails and two more attempts, I'd sent a text and then stopped trying. He must have still been with the police. Anyway, it looked like Lucas knocked the stalker's hand away; the gun went off; Lucas hit the guy in the chest and kicked him in the side of the knee, and as he started to collapse Lucas hit him again, in the face this time. Then he got hold of the gun hand and twisted. The gun dropped to the sidewalk. Meredith wrenched her arm free as the guy fell, and then both men were out of view. Meredith, instead of collapsing in a heap of screaming panic, bent and picked up the gun and pointed it at something out of the picture.

Yes, I watched the video more than once. The entire clip was less than ten seconds long. I thought Meredith deserved some kind of award for not shooting the creep.

I stepped away from the computer, thought about what I needed, took my phone through to the kitchen, and poured myself a glass of wine. I would have called Mom except I didn't want to tie up the line; Lucas might call. I really hoped he would. But more time passed, and still nothing.

It was close to midnight before the phone finally rang. I snatched it up and it was an unknown number. "Damn it!" I said out loud, but took a deep breath and connected because maybe he was using someone else's phone.

"Grace? It's me."

"Thank *God*. How are you? I saw a news report, well I said that in my message, but - " I closed my hands over the phone, held it away from my face and screamed across the room, then put the phone back where I could hear him. "Sorry. I've been waiting to scream until I knew you were really okay. You're okay, right?"

"I'm okay." He sounded like he was laughing, but in that shallow, kind of punchy, hysterical way you do when you've been under severe emotional stress. I heard him take a breath; it was a little shaky. "I'm really okay. It's been a hell of a day."

"I can't believe this all happened more than twenty-four hours ago and we're only now getting to talk. Ugh."

"Ugh is right."

"Tell me you broke his face."

"I broke his face. And a rib. The cops asked me why I hit him so hard."

"They asked you *WHY?!*"

He laughed again at my obvious outrage, and it sounded more normal this time. "His knee is fucked too. Good thing I kept up with the dojo, right? He was pretty much out cold when he went down."

"What happened after you stepped out of the picture?"

"Nothing, really. Meredith called 911, and then the show's security car showed up. She didn't let go of the gun until the police got there. A bunch of the neighbors came out and were milling around, but they were all scared so we didn't have to talk to them or anything."

I asked him to give me the sequence of events; he laid it out, and it sounded as though I'd gotten it pretty much in order. Then I asked, "Is your hand all right?"

"Hurts like hell. It's okay, nothing's broken. I don't have to play guitar for a couple of weeks."

"Oh my God Lucas. I wish I could come out there right now."

"I wish you could too."

"Is Meredith okay?"

"She spent half the night reaming out the cops for doing such a shitty job finding this guy, and not keeping an eye on the apartment complex, and ignoring the report she put in last year, and basically everything. She is full of righteous rage. I think she'll probably fall apart later, but she went to stay with a houseful of the girl dancers. They've got her."

That sounded like a good thing. "Are they pouring liquor down her throat?"

"Yeah, I think so."

"Did the show give you a couple days off, at least?"

"They offered. I took today, kind of didn't have a choice about that, but I'd rather get back to work. I don't want the schedule to get squirrelly, our thing in December might get messed up."

I realized there was a piece of the puzzle missing. "Did something happen to your phone?"

106

His voice got a little bit careful. "Yeah. Uh, don't freak out, but he shot it."

"He - when you did that block? Where was it?" My voice had gone squeaky.

"In my pocket. In my jacket."

"*Lucas*." I sat down on the floor and put my head on my knees.

"I am okay," he said, gently, as if he could see me. "I was not shot. But the phone is toast. Now it's in evidence. This is one the show sent me, that's why it took so long for me to get your messages. Well, that and having to tell the whole story to every damn body in the LVPD. And it wasn't only about last night, or the night before. It was everything I know about Meredith, everything she ever said about this guy - which until a couple days ago was nothing, to me at least - and every time I've ever spoken to her. I swear it was like they were trying to make a case that I was a homewrecker and the guy was justified coming after us." His words sped up and I could tell he was getting angry, maybe for the first time.

So was I. I leaned against the cabinet behind me, not ready to stand up again. "Well, he's a white guy, right? That must have been infuriating."

"Yeah. I think I didn't realize how mad I was getting. Which might be a good thing, because if I seemed mad they would think they were on the right track, right?"

Something occurred to me, which wouldn't have if it hadn't sounded like the cops were coming at this sideways. "Did you have a lawyer?"

"Yeah, the show's security team called someone and they had a lawyer there by the time we were taken back to the police station from the ER. That guy was taking some notes, let me tell you. He made it pretty clear he thought their whole approach was bullshit, demanded to see the evidence logs, everything. I don't think it's going to be a problem in the real world. But I have this feeling the press is going to try to make the story about me and Meredith stepping out." He sounded tired now.

"For what it's worth, I am confident that you and Meredith were not involved in any way, shape, or form except as co-workers."

"Well, thanks. I'm afraid you may have to say that to the media, sometime."

My problem-solving brain seemed to have engaged. "Is there someone in particular I should talk to? Someone you know, or at least someone you know is fair? What about that woman from Pop Quiz?"

"That's a good idea," he said, after a moment. "Sherry Martinez. Raquel knows her. Want me to tell Raquel that you'll give a statement but only to Sherry?"

"Yeah, that's fine." I couldn't think of anything else to say for a minute. I just wanted to hold him. I wanted to see him, and inspect him, and make sure he was really undamaged. "Lucas, I think I'm coming out there this weekend. I'll have to bring some work because exams are coming up, but otherwise it's three more weeks till I see you, and that's too long."

"I would love that," he said. He sounded so relieved I knew it was the right thing. "Send me your flight info and I'll meet you at the airport."

"I will do that. Talk to Raquel and if she thinks me doing a statement is advisable, maybe I can take care of it before the weekend. Either way, I'll see you in a few days. I'm so glad you're okay."

"Yeah. I might want to be an action hero on screen someday, but doing it in real life is not so fun."

Incredibly, I laughed. "Maybe you should put that security footage in your reel." He didn't say anything right away. "Too soon?" Then I realized he was laughing, and was finally able to get back on my feet. I listened, smiling, until he ran down. "Are you at home?"

"Yeah," he said, still sounding a bit giggly.

"Have a big drink or something and go to sleep. That's what I'm going to do. I love you."

"I love you too. Can't wait to see you."

He didn't need to put it in his reel. It was all over the internet the next day. And honestly, it was impressive, at least once I was able to look at it objectively. A block, three strikes, and the gun-wielding madman goes down. It made all those long, drawn-out on-screen fights I'd seen seem faintly ridiculous. Before firmly putting it out of my mind, because I did have school stuff to do, I watched it one more time and thought *that's what it looks like when he doesn't pull his punch, bitches*. I drove down to campus still grinning at how politically incorrect it was to be proud of him for such successful violence.

By Friday I'd talked to Mom, Luisa, and Raquel about the whole situation and was - if possible - even more proud of Lucas. He was conducting himself so steadily. There was a mob of press at the soundstage when he got there the day after we talked. He had to give multiple press statements, with patient repetition of the bare facts, as well as of the fact that he and Meredith were simply co-workers, neighbors, and friends. There was news and 'news' about the whole affair, and sure enough, as he'd started to suspect, some people wanted to rewrite the story to make it all Lucas' fault. Meredith did her best to put a stop to that, pointing out that she'd filed reports on the ex before and that he had violent priors (which the police confirmed). Raquel set me up with Sherry just in case, and it did come to a point where my statement was released. On the plane to Las Vegas Friday night, I saw that they'd even gone to Sharysse.

After watching her statement, I could totally get why Lucas had fallen for her back in the day. She was really pretty, for one thing; chocolate-skinned, shapely, with intelligent eyes and a luscious mouth that reminded me of Ray. And she stood up for Lucas. When a reporter tried to insinuate that he was a womanizer, Sharysse shut it down instantly. She said, "Lucas was a faithful husband. I have no doubt that he is faithful to his new fiancée. For you to imply that he wasn't, or isn't, makes me wonder about your agenda."

Then the reporter - a woman; I hated that it was a woman playing this angle - asked who was at fault in the divorce. Sharysse said baldly, "I was. I got married one month after the divorce was final. My baby was born seven months after that. You do the math. If you're capable," and I squealed a little bit.

Lucas was there at the airport when I got past the secure area, and there were press people hanging around, but I didn't care. I kissed him anyway. "Did you see the thing with Sharysse? I want to send her flowers." He laughed, and showed me his phone; he'd had the story up too. "How's Meredith?"

"She's doing well. She wants to meet you. Is that okay?"

"Absolutely." He picked up my weekender and slung it over his shoulder. I caught a glimpse of his right hand; it looked a little swollen, and the knuckles were discolored.

He noticed my attention. "The ER guy said he was surprised nothing was broken. Then I told him about b-boying, and martial arts, and he said Oh." I laughed. Lucas had big, tough, square hands. I'd always liked them; they looked, in Sharysse's word, capable. And I could vouch for how strong they were.

McCarran is a small airport compared to LAX. We were out and into the waiting taxi before I knew it. "So I had to bring a bunch of reading. What's on your schedule this weekend?"

"I have a four-hour call tomorrow, then I'm done till four on Monday. If you have time, I have something to show you."

"A sneak peek?"

"Yeah, kind of. I had this great talk with Kathy, the head writer," he said. "Remember I told you we had a deportation storyline?"

"Uh-huh."

"Well, when I told her about this song I wanted to use, it was for this episode where the U.S. citizen half of the couple decides to leave the country so she can be with her boyfriend who was sent back to Panama. She didn't quite see it at first because she thought I was talking about doing it as a single scene, and I'm barely in the episode. But I was thinking we score the episode with it. Like, you almost want to not realize it's me singing. Because it's not about my character at all, it's about Stephanie and how much she's willing to give up. There was all this stuff for Steph to do, but she didn't have dialogue for it because she's all alone, right?"

"And she's a non-singing part. Gotcha. So they were going to use random music? Huh. You have some rehearsal footage?"

"Just me playing it. And you can read the script if you want."

"Sure. We could do that tonight."

"We have something else to do first," he said, and I laughed. "Kathy said if the team likes the way it comes out, we might cut together another video single. 'A Little Less Conversation' went over well."

"Of course it did, you looked amazing. You *sounded* amazing." We pulled up at the apartment gate. Lucas handed his access card to the driver, who used it to activate the gate, then handed it back to Lucas and drove in. Either he knew the complex really well or Lucas had already given him instructions. We were dropped off and got upstairs fast, and as soon as the door was locked behind us Lucas started kissing me. He didn't stop for quite a while.

"Okay," I said eventually. "I am now satisfied that you are undamaged. And also generally." I stretched luxuriously and started looking around for my clothes.

He got out of bed, grinning, and brought me a robe. "Are you hungry?"

"Yes. Is there food?"

"I picked up some stuff earlier. Didn't want to waste time cooking."

"Good, neither do I." We went to the living area, which included the small kitchen. Lucas hadn't been kidding about the place being not too big. There was enough space to prepare food, eat, watch TV, and sleep, plus a bathroom and a spacious closet. He told me that the complex had a gym, a pool, and laundry facilities, as well as a common room the residents could use for gatherings. Almost like a good dormitory. Apparently that space got quite a workout; over the course of the weekend, as we went in and out, I saw several different groups using it. I approved; it kept noise out of the actual living spaces pretty well.

After we ate, Lucas woke up his laptop to play me the video of him doing the song in a rehearsal room, with only the guitar. I hadn't heard the song before; it was called 'Today, Tomorrow and Forever.' It was slow, quiet, almost melancholy, and utterly lovely. "Jeez, Lucas," I said, "it's a good thing you played this for me now or I would have been totally bawling at your taping." He handed me a tissue.

"I about cried the first time I really listened to it," he admitted. "The first time I heard it I was driving, but I remembered the title. I found a bunch of versions, we're not the only ones who like it. I thought … ."

"What?"

He gave me a long look, and there was so much love in his expression that I almost started crying for real. "I thought it would be a great wedding song."

"I love you so much," I said. So then there was some more kissing. A little later I asked, "Are you going to do it like that, with only the guitar?"

"Nancy's going to play the bass, like she did on 'Love Me Tender,' with me on the guitar. That's all."

"Let me see the script." He brought it over, handed it to me with a kiss, and cleaned up the kitchen while I read it. Going in with a sense of his vision, I couldn't imagine that Stephanie's scenes would have worked with random music. I mean, okay, they would have worked; the episode was well written. But not nearly as well as they would work with that song as the leitmotif. The last scene was when she got off the bus in Panama and her boyfriend was there. There wasn't going to be a dry eye when people watched it.

113

When I set the script aside, Lucas sat down beside me. I said, "I'm not surprised Kathy is going with your idea. It's going to be great."

"I'm glad you think so. You're kind of my ideal audience." I must have looked surprised. "I mean, you pay attention to music and theater, and film. You don't just sit and let stuff wash over you."

"Neither do you. You need to give yourself more credit." I regarded him for a minute. "Or not. Stay all humble and sweet like this, so when you take down the bad guys in ten seconds everyone is like whoa." He laughed.

"Raquel asked me if I wanted her to find me an action thing for next summer."

"What did you say?"

"I said if I got what I wanted, I was going to see plenty of action in New Zealand." He leaned over and kissed me.

It was a good thing he had to report in for a while on Saturday. Otherwise I might have fallen severely behind with my study schedule. As it was, between dinner with Meredith Saturday night and some more damage-testing on Sunday, I only logged about seven hours of reading. It meant I'd have to really buckle down once I got home. But I didn't regret it for a second.

The week after the whole crazy incident, because some of the press was still really stupid, the show's lawyer got into the evidence room with a sergeant and a local reporter who wasn't stupid. He gave a short speech about the stalker's history of violence and his history with Meredith. He pointed out that both incidents had been captured on security video and there wasn't any legitimate question about who was the aggressor. Then he held up my black leather jacket with light behind it to show the bullet hole through the side, front and back, saying, "The only reason Mr. Gutierrez wasn't shot is because he took action to defend himself." He put the jacket on. It was frighteningly clear that if I hadn't been moving in pretty much exactly the way I'd been moving - which is to say, blocking with my left hand and striking with my right - the bullet would have gone into my chest. "Any questions?" The reporter, of course, didn't have any because the whole thing was a set-up. But it was an effective piece of theatre.

I sent the clip to Grace and got a reply by text: *I like that guy. And I love you*. I also sent it to Kate at the dojo in L.A., with the security footage and a note: *your training*. I laughed at what she wrote back: *glad it works*.

The show sent me a new jacket. Meredith and I didn't miss any work days. Social media for 'Behind the Strip' was going nuts; they'd had to hire a second person to handle everything. Part of her job was screening posts that showed me and Meredith together. It seemed like everyone in Las Vegas had taken pictures. There were some that showed us out on Gate Night where Derek and Kelly had been clumsily cropped or Photoshopped out of the picture, trying to make it look like Meredith and I were out alone. The screener, Angie, through some kind of magic - I'll never understand it - found the original images and posted them with increasingly snarky comments in response each time she found one of the doctored pictures. It got so by the second week of December, every time we heard someone laughing around the set, we assumed it was Angie at work again. I knew Grace was following the Twitter and Instagram feeds because after a particularly good zinger, I got a text that said *BAHAHA.*

I wrote back *She works here in LV, want to meet her when you come out again? She makes me feel old*

Is she like eighteen?

Yep. Ready for exams?

Have to tell you it's a good thing I pretty much know this stuff because my study habits are in the garbage

You'll be fine. How many job offers now

LOL four

I was impressed. I mean, I knew how brilliant she was, but there's always that 'what if.' *Anything tempting?*

Yeah but I'm holding out. Still another semester, gaahh. Can't wait to see you again

Same here. Gotta get back to work. I love you

I love you too

Julia and my parents got to town on the thirteenth. My folks had decided to take some long-overdue vacation since they hadn't been to Vegas for years. They all knew I was working long hours wrapping up some scenes before the production shut down for the winter break, so we didn't try to set up a dinner or anything, only exchanged texts and calls. Julia took my folks out to see a Cirque du Soleil show that night.

On the fourteenth, Grace sent another text that said *ON MY WAY*. She'd already given me her incoming flight information, but Julia was going to pick her up at the airport. I got done with my long day - twelve hours of short bits to fill in or refine previously-taped scenes - at eight o'clock and immediately texted Grace: *finally done. Did I miss dinner?*

Yeah but the gang's all here and wants to see you anyway. We're up in Mom's suite and there might be champagne

LOL wish I didn't have to work tomorrow. Stop me at one glass

Two more days right? Do Luisa and Cesar know what song you're doing?

No it'll be a surprise

OK I'll make sure and bring a box of tissues. Now get over here! Text me so I can meet you at the elevator and do some kissing without parents watching

LMAO will do. I was there in less than half an hour. Grace met me, as promised. We made it into Julia's room about ten minutes later.

My parents were used to me being gone for pretty long stretches, but with everything that had happened, there was a little more hugging than usual. Julia got in on that action, too. "I was so impressed," she said after we'd all talked for a while. "I mean, I was horrified, but you really handled yourself well. And Meredith!"

"She was great," I agreed. "She said she didn't want the guy to do what all the bad guys do in the movies, you know, and all of a sudden grab the gun again."

"God, no," said my mother. "She was so brave."

"She's still here, right?" Grace asked. "Do you think she'd be able to join us for dinner tomorrow?"

"Let's see." I sent a quick text. "My day's supposed to be short, since we're doing the song on-set, nothing fancy. The director scheduled three hours and said if it looked good on the monitors they'd probably cut me and Nancy loose. The next day's still scheduled for cleanup but it shouldn't be as long as today."

My mother said, "I can't wait to see it. I remember when you used to sing all the time around the house."

"He did?" Grace said, giving me a sideways look.

"Oh yes. Before his voice changed, he used to do Michael Jackson."

"Mama!"

Grace laughed. "Oh my God Lucas you should see your face right now. Really?"

I knew I was blushing. "Tell me you don't have video of any of that anymore, Mama, please."

"Tell me you *do*!" said Grace. "The dances and everything?"

"Everything," said my dad. I had my head in my hands, laughing. Dad went on, "That's why when we moved, and the performing-arts school was right on the same street, we took him down there."

"Lucas told me about that school. He's lucky it was there."

"And a police station was at the end of the block," Mama put in. "I wish we'd lived there always."

"I do too, Mama," I said. "You had some tough times."

"All of us did. But everything's good now." She changed the subject then, asking Grace about graduate school, and then we got to talking about Julia's new job up in Minneapolis.

Just when I was thinking I'd have to go home, my phone buzzed with a reply from Meredith. I read it and told everybody, "Meredith can join us for dinner tomorrow. She's free after four, says let her know where to meet us."

"That'll be great. I want to ask her if that lawyer made a move yet," Grace said. "I could tell he liked her."

"You're matchmaking," Julia said. "That's not like you."

"Well, you know," Grace said, glancing at me, "there's only one Lucas, but there are a lot of guys out there who are not actually creeps. Meredith deserves one of those."

"We all do," said Julia. "I got lucky twice. Your dad called me again, by the way."

"Oh yeah? Is he trying to get you back again?"

"He might be. Trying, I mean."

I was watching this little volley, as were my parents, not sure if either Julia or Grace thought that was a good thing. It was almost exactly a year since Julia and Ray had gotten married, right here in Las Vegas. She seemed okay, but ... . For now, I had to call it a day. "Well, I've got to report in by eight again for makeup so I'd better get going. You've got the directions to the soundstage, right?"

"We've got 'em. Let me walk you out," said Grace, ignoring her mother's laugh. I did another round of hugs and then we left the suite. I put my arm around her and she pressed close. I waited till we'd turned the corner to kiss her. "I wish I could come home with you tonight," Grace said after a while.

"I wish you could too. Maybe tomorrow. Your mom doing okay?"

"She said she had a moment when she got here, but that trip last year is such a good memory. She said she's so glad they had that. And God, so am I. I'm so glad they got married." She kissed me again. "How long do you want me to stay?"

I gave her a long look, as if I had to think about it. "Forever." She laughed. "But I guess it would be hard for you to finish your degree from here. So, as long as you can." I kissed her again. "I love you."

"I love you too. Go get some rest." She walked backward down the hall until she had to turn the corner, then blew me a kiss and disappeared.

The next day, Nancy and I were on set and ready a little bit early. We'd rehearsed several different approaches to the song, and I'd discussed them with Kathy and the director. The plan was to tape five different versions. They'd make a decision about which one - or which combination - to use after they got to the editing room. We warmed up a little, then I went for a walk around the soundstage, snooping on what other folks were doing while I waited for my guests to arrive. When they did, I took them all around to the small seating area that the crew had set up behind the camera line.

We were lucky, because almost everything else was done; another set was booked, but nothing would be shot until after we were finished for the day. I told the family what we were doing. "There are going to be kind of long breaks between each version, for the director to have a look at the playback. And we may go back and re-take things, so it might get a little boring for you. But, you know, welcome to TV, right Julia?"

"So right," she said. "I noticed there is coffee down the hall."

"And you will need it," I said, which made Dad and Mama laugh. "I'll see you all again in a while. If it gets too bad just take off, my feelings won't be hurt."

Mama said, "Estás loco," and Dad laughed again. I knew they wouldn't leave. I was counting on it.

For the first take I used my natural voice, which was closer to Mexico than to Graceland. I was making an effort not to make eye contact with anybody behind the camera line - the lights helped with that - but I thought there was a little bit of reaction. My guitar part on this one was the most complicated of any of the versions. Nancy's bass line had a smooth rumba rhythm, and she tapped a syncopation on the frets of the bass. It was the most modern version of the song. The break to review playback went pretty fast, and the director didn't ask for a retake.

The next take was in my Elvis voice. My guitar part was simplified, and Nancy had more to do on the bass. I was pretty happy with that one, but after playback the director asked me to do it again "with more Elvis, like, *all* the Elvis" so after we got done laughing I went to town on it.

Then we did two instrumental takes. The first one had the guitar doing melody, and the second time Nancy played the 'voice.' I liked that one a lot. She was a damn good bass player; she could make it sound like a drum or a cello or a mountain lion when she wanted. There weren't any comments or retakes on those.

Finally we got to my big secret version. I hoped Grace really had brought a box of tissues because I thought they were going to need it. With the mic live and tape running, I said, "This one is for Luisa and

Cesar." Nancy and I started to play, and then I sang 'Today, Tomorrow and Forever' in my show-Elvis voice, but in Spanish.

I'd had to get help from another Spanish-speaker in the cast, because I couldn't find a translation that I liked and my own Spanish was sketchy after so many years doing English-only jobs. Mama told me later that it was just right. Well, she would, wouldn't she? Turned out that was the one they used for the episode.

When we were all done and they cut me and Nancy loose, I brought her to meet the family. Mama was still sniffling. I didn't even say anything, only hugged her. Dad joined in, then Grace. Pretty soon it was everybody.

"So it was a good thing Grace brought those tissues, right?" I said after a while, which got a laugh. I introduced Nancy, we all chatted for a while, and then the set manager came over to kick us out because someone else was about to start taping.

It was great to spend the whole afternoon and evening with family. I wasn't sure if it was because I was getting older, or because I was in love, but I was really not looking forward to being alone once Grace had to go back to L.A. The longest she could reasonably stay was till New Years. When we had a minute to ourselves, I said, "I think I'll come back with you to L.A. after Christmas. There's no need for me to be here."

"I was hoping you'd say that," she said. "There's a lot of people in L.A. who want to see you, too."

"Are you keeping up with what the Underground Cabaret is doing?"

"Not really. They did release the schedule and the themes for 2018 though."

"Oh yeah? I must have missed that email."

"It came in a couple of weeks ago," she said, giving me the side-eye. "You were a little busy."

"I'll go dig for it. I kind of feel like I want to do something again. The dance we do here on the show is fun, but it's not all me, you know?"

"Well, is June even possible for you to pull off, with all this going on? I think the theme was 'On the Edge.' They're looking for dances using music about California. But like I said, I haven't really talked to anyone about it."

"Oh, man. I've *already* got an idea. But maybe not for a solo. And if I do something in June what're we gonna do about New Zealand? Shit."

She laughed. "We can always go to New Zealand after the show. We should invite everybody over while you're in town. We'll figure it out."

All I wanted in that moment was to be alone with her, skin to skin. It would reinforce that feeling that I never wanted us to be apart, which meant being apart would suck even more; but the more time we spent together the more sure I was that, eventually, we would get there for good. "Can you come home with me tonight? I don't have to report in till ten tomorrow."

"Pretty sure Mom will be okay with that." She kissed me and headed over to check in with Julia. I kept half an eye on their conversation while I was talking to Mama. It looked like we got the all-clear. Julia led a general movement toward the door after a while, and we got ourselves together for the evening.

At dinner, Grace did ask Meredith about the lawyer. For a second she seemed embarrassed, because we were all looking interested and that was definitely in the category of 'getting all up in your business,' but then she sighed, smiling, and said, "There might have been a

123

conversation where he said he had to keep his distance, because I'm a witness if this thing goes to trial. So he said he's hoping John makes a plea deal." Grace and Julia got it right away and started laughing. The rest of us caught up pretty fast.

For all that the family day had been great, it was so good to close the door behind us, only the two of us. Grace seemed to feel the same way. We didn't need any words for a long time. When we were finally too exhausted to do anything else, and she was lying beside me with her head on my shoulder, I said, "So did you get pretty tired of that song?"

"I'll never be tired of that song," she said, and kissed me one more time.

VII - Grace
December 2017

It was nice having family time, though I will confess I felt guilty about Dad being alone in Los Angeles while I was with all these other people. (Though I was also really glad that all these other people were on hand to help distract Mom from what should have been her anniversary.) I really wondered about him and Mom sometimes. Their divorce had been about as amicable as a divorce involving a child and property could be, but there had been some weirdness when Mom met Ray. First, I think, because he was so much younger than she was; but also, undoubtedly, because he was black. (Well, mixed-race; but we all know what that means in America.)

There were plenty of interracial couples in our circle of acquaintance. L.A. is full of them. But things can look different when it's suddenly someone you're close to.

Anyway, he appeared to have gotten over most of that. And maybe now he thought he might step back in. He hadn't remarried, and I'd noticed when we got together after Japan that he looked really fit. If he wanted to try, I wasn't going to discourage him, even though I thought Mom might break his heart again. We'd all learned by now that love hurts.

Fortunately, Lucas and I had a little over three weeks in which love was perfect. I stayed in Las Vegas with him until the day after Christmas. There was absolutely nothing we had to do, which seemed very strange to both of us. We saw a few shows, we spent time with some of Lucas' local friends, we went out dancing. We talked a lot, about my situation and his situation and how we might deal with things. And on

Christmas I let him read the email I wrote after his declaration.

> Lucas Gutierrez. You do it to me every time. I think I've figured you out, and then you come up with something that makes me recalibrate. It's very good training for a baby engineer.
>
> I thought you'd write me a nice long letter about 'God.' But you were smart enough to know you didn't need to. Everything you needed to say about it was right there. Did you trust me to read it right? I guess with all the years of watching Mom and the others dance their stories, I should be able to. But that's something else we haven't talked about, so it must have been trust.
>
> I wonder if you have any idea how much I trust you. I'm not even sure where it started. Probably with that first day when we danced, and it was perfect, and then when the whole world could probably tell I was ready to fall for you, you were honest and gentle and didn't make me feel like an idiot.
>
> It's probably also, at least a little bit, because I know Ray trusted you. He was a smart guy, he didn't let liking someone turn off his judgement. That's a thing Mom loved about him.
>
> Have you always been good at letters? Because I have to tell you, you're kind of acing it. I've tried that gambit before, you know, "Tell me about," and every guy but you has used it as a platform for his opinions and a springboard for demands. You've told me what you know, not only what you want, or what you believe.

And I read back over this, because I've been writing it for a couple of days now, and I see what I just wrote, "you've told me what you know," and then I look back at your message and I think *that means he knows he loves me*, and it's all I can do not to get on the phone right now (yes of course I have your number, it was in Ray's phone, and it kills me to write that because I know you miss him at least as much as I do) and tell you I love you too.

Grace Hart

Watching him read it made me cry. We were both looking for tissues for a few minutes there. After we got ourselves in order he said, "That's a really good letter."

"Thanks, I worked on it." He laughed. "So tell me about you and letters."

"I don't think I ever wrote a real letter in my life, until you asked me to tell you about the show."

"No, really?" That was a little hard to believe.

"Yeah. I mean, emails and stuff, sure. But like business stuff. Or casual notes. It was always more about phone calls or texts. I liked writing the letters."

"Well, I thought you must have, or you wouldn't have kept doing it. And honestly, as gorgeous and as talented as you are, if you hadn't done it so well I could have, like, cured myself."

He smiled and gave me a sideways look, like oh really? "I used yours for a model. I tried to analyze it, like, why did she put things in this order, how does this work for the flow. I thought the whole thing was … an invitation? For me to communicate with you on your terms. It was a challenge, too."

"I was looking for a reason not to be crazy about you. Because the career thing scares me."

He nodded, accepting that. We'd talked about it before. "Maybe we'll get lucky and I'll get a gig like Ray's that shoots in L.A."

"Once I'm working the budget will open up a little, I'll be able to come out here more often. Dad paid for my tickets when I told him what happened, he said I could use the emergency credit card. He's paid for my school. Mom's still paying the expenses for the house, since she's living with Granddad and she basically doesn't have any living expenses. I mean to say," I said seriously, "I am, at present, a kept woman."

He laughed again. "I figured it was none of my business about money on your side, until we're actually married. Do I need to get ready to make a case to your dad that I can support you?"

"Gross, no. I mean, it'll make him happy to know you *could*."

"Well, I could," he said.

"Great. But once I'm working I'll be making decent money." The offers I'd already gotten were proof of that. "I'll take over the house expenses in Los Angeles. You might have to pay for that honeymoon in New Zealand."

"I've been counting on that. Why do you think this apartment is so damn small?"

I laughed like a fool for a solid minute. "I mean, we could wait a while to get married and do the honeymoon. But I don't think either of us really wants to. Wait, I mean."

"I absolutely don't want to wait." He pulled me close again and kissed me. "So are we driving back to L.A. tomorrow? In my sad old shot-up car?"

"Oh my God, you haven't even had a chance to get the windows replaced, huh?" Did I feel guilty about that? No, no I didn't. We deserved some time to Not Deal With Stuff.

"I could have taken the time but I had something more important to do." He was still holding me tight. "I can get that done in about a minute in L.A. It's big business over there."

I swear he cracked me up sometimes. But you know, he was right.

The only thing interesting about the drive from Las Vegas to Los Angeles (or vice versa) is the mental odds-making about whether that car squatting in the left lane is going to stay there or whether it's going to GTFO of the way. It is a desolate stretch of road. We left pretty early so that we could get into the city without the sun glaring in our eyes. I pretended not to notice the bullet holes in the car (which was kind of hard since the perforated windows whistled the whole way). Someone had put a fake-leather 'Bad Motherfucker' sticker over the hole in the dashboard since the last time I'd seen it. I'd been mentally giggling over it all day. "Was that you?" I asked, finally, as Lucas pulled into my driveway.

"No, Meredith put that there," he said, smiling. "She said she tried to find a wallet, you know, like Jules' in 'Pulp Fiction,' but she couldn't so she settled for this."

"This works. I didn't tell you," I said, before we got out of the car, "I had this, like, atavistic reaction to seeing you take that guy down. Totally cavewoman. I was all yeah, bitches, that's my man."

He laughed, and leaned over to kiss me. "So it didn't scare you?"

"The *incident* scared me. *You* did not scare me. *You* turned me on even more than you usually do."

129

"Let's hope it still works when I'm only faking it." He was still in reach, so I kissed him again, then remembered we could now go in the house and do other things, if we were so inclined. (We usually were. Mom had told me this phase might last quite a while, and that we should enjoy it to the fullest. We were taking that advice.) We both got out of the car and I went to open the door while he got our bags and his guitar case out of the trunk, saying, "If I do that project next summer ... ."

Raquel had sent a wheedling email about a summer TV-movie project she wanted Lucas to take. He hadn't even been asked to audition; it was an up-front offer. But he wanted a little time to make up his mind. The 'Behind the Strip' buyer hadn't yet committed to further production, and the cast might not find out until after both new 13-episode runs were complete. Fitting in an Underground Cabaret show, a wedding, a honeymoon, *and* a movie might be pushing it if 'Strip' ended up going back into production earlier than October. On the other hand, it was a movie, with a very different role for Lucas, and the bit of script we'd gotten a look at didn't suck.

On the *other* other hand, the project was going to be filmed in Vancouver. "If you do it, you'll be great, but I have to be honest and say I hope something else comes along."

"Yeah. Well, let's not make a decision right away. I'll tell her I'd rather have something local."

We spent the next couple of days taking care of business. Lucas went to see Raquel and talk about how things were going in Las Vegas, and got the work done on his car. I set up a dinner for us with Dad, and started editing an article some teammates and I were going to submit to a couple of the major civil engineering journals. We'd had time to do most of the research and writing during the fall semester, but with my upcoming internship in mind, I needed to get it off my desk now.

Dad grilled Lucas a little at dinner. It wasn't too bad, really. Lucas had been working steadily for so long that his stability (a.k.a. 'future employability in notoriously fickle entertainment industry') wasn't really in question. Plus I could brandish my job offers. As I told Dad, I fully expected to get another one from Jerry Weiss at the end of my second internship with him. "And that's the one I'll probably accept," I said. "I like Jerry, and he's kind of part of the family. I've known Sharon and Vicky almost since they started at Dmitri's." Sharon was Jerry's daughter, and Vicky was Sharon's wife. They'd both gotten Latin ballroom coaching from Mom.

"Well, make sure it's a fair offer," Dad said. "I know being right here in town is worth something, but still."

"Yeah, I know." I recited the formula he had drilled into me after watching female associates in his firm accept lower starting rates than men, and never catch up. "The lower the price I accept at the beginning, the lower my lifetime earnings will be." There had been a time when I'd considered law school, but that was before Fukushima. For some reason that event had really grabbed me.

Anyway, it was a good dinner. My men seemed to get along. We cooked at home (to prove we could) and then showed Dad a couple of episodes of 'Behind the Strip.' "I guess I'll have to watch the whole thing now," he said, which made Lucas laugh. "And I guess I should get back to Las Vegas sometime. It looks completely different from the last time I was there."

"When was that, anyway?" I asked.

"Oh, before you were born."

"Holy moly, Dad. No wonder it looks different."

"If you come out, I could introduce you to some people," said Lucas. "There's a lot going on in Vegas right now. I know some of my cast mates don't have lawyers yet. The only reason I have one is I was friends with Ray, and he badgered me about it."

Dad laughed at that. "A lot of you young talents get screwed because you do good work early on and don't get properly compensated. Or even credited, sometimes. Ray was right. Did he badger you about life insurance, too?"

"Yeah, he did." Lucas glanced over at me. That was something we *hadn't* talked about.

"It's made a big difference for Julia." He didn't pursue it; Dad was getting better about not turning a casual conversational point into a lecture. And after that, he wound up the evening quite neatly by suggesting we do a Sunday brunch before Lucas had to go back to work. We liked the idea, so he said he would set that up and send us the details. Then he and Lucas shook hands, and I walked him out to his car.

"So, what do you think," I said after the door closed behind us.

"I like him. I'm glad he's a little older than you. You're too bright for a man your own age." I laughed, but he shook his head. "I'm serious. Men are too ego-driven when they're young," he said. "I'm a prime example."

"You had to be ego-driven to get where you wanted to be. So did Lucas. He's still got a pretty strong ego."

"Of course, but now he's also got quite a history of success. It doesn't seem like he's going to be threatened when *you* succeed. He's not going to want you to say no to opportunities just because what you're doing isn't all about him."

I knew he wasn't talking about me and Lucas at this point, but I pretended he was. "I don't think he did that with Sharysse, either. But I know what you mean. I'm glad you like him."

"And I'm glad." He seemed to stall, looking away for a moment. "This is really old-world. I'm glad to know he's a man who could, and would, protect you." I patted his shoulder. "So what do you think of middle-aged white guys who get tattoos?" That made me laugh. One of the episodes we'd played had shown off Lucas' Quetzalcoatl in all, and I do mean *all*, its glory. Lucas blushed all the way through watching that scene; I don't think he remembered, when we chose the episode, that he was mostly naked in it. (I, of course, remembered *every* episode where he was mostly naked.)

"Um," I said to Dad, "it depends on where the tattoo goes, doesn't it?" He laughed, and kissed me goodnight, and got in the car. I waved as he drove away. Then I went back inside to my fiancé, helped him finish cleaning up the kitchen, and took him to bed.

The next day was one of those luxurious days of having no external demands. We always had stuff to do, but we didn't have to go anywhere. Lucas did his thing while I did mine. I could hear music, as usual. We checked in with each other at midday, fetching up in the kitchen without planning to and sitting down to eat lunch together. I could tell Lucas felt more at home in the house now than he did in the fall. Having him there made it feel more like home. Not simply the place I was living. When we met up again for dinner I asked him if there was anything about the house that he wanted to change. He looked so surprised that I had to clarify. "I want to make sure you feel like this is your home too. Not like you're a guest, or whatever. I know it must feel a little weird when so much of your life is in Las Vegas."

He gave me a thoughtful look. "The thing is," he said, "I haven't had a place that was really home. My place with Sharysse came close, but half the time I wasn't there. She was in charge of that place. It didn't occur to me to have an opinion."

"You?" I let the doubt show in my tone. He smiled. "Well, in that case, you know what I mean. You don't have to have an opinion about it. If everything here works for you, great. But if you ever *do* have an opinion, I'm here on the record saying speak up, okay?"

"Okay." After a second: "I'll think about it."

I was right about one thing: we needed those extra days together. When I thought about how much of our relationship had been spent apart, the six months stretching ahead of us looked endless. I was already making plans to come back to L.A. during the production's spring break.

One thing that was now very clear was that being in the same room was awfully helpful when it came to making decisions. I should have expected that, right? So much of my trouble with Sharysse had been based on the same thing: distance. I realized that Grace and I both had a tendency to be noncommittal in our emails or texts. If one person didn't clearly have strong feelings about something, we both kind of hung back. But when I could see her face, and she could see mine, it was so much easier to tell when somebody cared more (or less) about something. By the end of that winter break we'd had the opportunity to see that in action enough that I thought we'd do better, even at a distance, going forward. We agreed that we would make some kind of contact every day. We also agreed to try FaceTime. I'd only ever done it for work-related stuff, and she'd never done it at all.

Neither of us wanted to do some big New Year's Eve going-out thing, but we wanted to see a whole lot of people, so Grace suggested inviting pretty much everyone we knew in L.A. to a New Year's Day open house. We stocked up on food and beverages, and told people to come whenever.

We were expecting quite a few of the Underground Cabaret people to drop in. I knew a lot of them. Principals Michelle and Paula both danced in 'Face the Music;' their partner Rory was one of the stage managers. I'd been in touch to find out if anyone had claimed 'Hotel California' for the June show. Rory wrote back: *I was planning to submit something. Do you have an idea? Because I would totes work with you.*

Hey Rory, yeah, in fact my idea was kind of riffing on your thing in 'Cosmic' last summer. I didn't get a chance to fully appreciate at the time but after I saw the video, just wow

TYVM. I liked your thing too. Let's talk soon

So I was hoping Rory and her wife Dana would come to our open house. Rory had done a jazz piece set to Madonna's 'Human Nature' that really rang my bell. If she thought we could work together, I was more than willing.

By the end of that day, we were good to go. Obviously Rory knew me already. She came through the door saying the same thing she said when we first met: "Aren't you a little tall for a b-boy?" Before I could even answer she followed that up with "Do you have rehearsal space in Las Vegas?"

I said, like I did before, "B-boys and stormtroopers come in all sizes." She gave me a thumbs-up. "Yeah, I've got a line on a couple different spaces. So what do you think?"

"My wife says I can go over there to work with you. She might even come with me if I play my cards right."

"I know all about TV schedules," said Dana, smiling. "I'm on 'Ten-31' right now."

"Yeah, Ray told me when you joined the cast. I still watch it."

"Do you like it?"

"Needs more dancing," I said seriously, and she snorted out a laugh. They stayed for quite a while; Rory and I went back to Julia's practice room and brainstormed for a half hour while Grace and Dana talked with some others who'd shown up, including Paula and her husband Mike. When we got done we were both pretty sure our ideas would mesh. We joined the others and I said, "Thanks for loaning me Rory. She's threatening me with lifts, though. So maybe Mike needs to come out to LV once or twice, too."

"Well, he's the one to ask," said Dana. I knew that was true – the things Mike and Paula did were unreal. Mike said he'd be happy to, and Paula muttered something about finding a song for *them* to use. We talked some more about dance stuff, which fortunately didn't bore Grace, and then more people showed up who had feet in both the TV and dance worlds. I had a moment of thinking *this is so cool*, because now all these people were my people, and not only because we were on a job together.

"So we got this message from Tanith Salazar," said this one guy, Andy, a former Broadway dancer, more recently a photographer, and currently a featured actor on 'L.A. Vice.' Not everybody seemed to know who he was talking about. I certainly didn't. "She's making a movie next summer."

"No kidding!" said Rory. "We only really met her the one time, when we were stage-managing 'Green Darkness.' What's the movie about?"

"Carlos Gardel, the Argentine tango singer. She wants Victor to play the lead, and I'll be doing something. She's looking to cast the rest of it pretty soon. The reason I bring it up here is she wants a ton of dancers, but there's three other male singing roles."

"Where is she filming?" Grace asked, looking over at me. I knew next to nothing about tango, but any kind of musical project had my attention.

"Here in L.A. There's going to be theater scenes, and milonga scenes, and street scenes like in 'Evita' with all the dance extras."

"You should nudge Raquel," Grace told me. "See if she can get you the script."

I definitely wanted to do that. "Better than Vancouver, huh?"

"You know Raquel?" Andy asked, like there was only one Raquel in L.A., but at the moment it seemed inevitable. "She's my agent."

"Mine too," I said, laughing a little, thinking *small world*. Andy got his phone out and started texting somebody. His husband Victor was sitting there laughing too. I raised my eyebrows in a question and he nodded.

"Yeah, he's texting her. We stumbled on your show not long ago and now I can't get him to stop watching it."

"I need Lucas for the thing! I'm prepping a show," Andy said to me. "I never thought I'd get my hands on you. I mean, I saw you in 'The Great Wave' but at the time I was doing another thing, and our girls were moving in, and then you were *gone* and I couldn't chase you down because we were so crazed. And then last year I was being a Victor groupie out of town most of the summer. I was here for a minute to do the promo shots for 'Face the Music' and I was, like, gnashing my teeth."

"Not an exaggeration," said Victor.

"I chose you," Andy told him, "like I always do. But I was *bitter*."

I was laughing for real now, along with pretty much everyone else. "I'm here in L.A. till the end of the week."

"Let's make a date!" So we talked a bit about his current project and found a gap in his schedule. He sent me the address of his home studio later, in an email, with a link to his website so I could see some of his other work.

"Are there any of these people who aren't super-talented?" I asked Grace that night, after looking through all that (and almost going down the rabbit hole of links for his subjects, some of whom I'd come to know).

"I have a theory about that," she said. "Which is that people who are very good at one thing can often be very good at a bunch of things, and it's simply down to luck whether they open the right doors. You know, which cabinet is which talent in. Mom originally was an actress. Then she became a dancer. Now she's a teacher. She's good at all of it. And, I mean, look at someone like Eddie Murphy. He's a great comic, but he's a great actor, he can really sing, and I'll bet he can dance, too."

"He was so good in 'Dreamgirls.'"

"His songs are basically the only ones I ever listen to from that soundtrack. Anyway, you fit right in with this gang, don't worry. I'm glad you're going to do this thing with Andy. He did that portrait of Ray that's in the dining room." It was the picture they'd had on display at the memorial, taken during the 'Gaucho' tango show. "He did some really nice ones of Ray and Mom together, too."

"Think he'd do wedding pictures for us?"

"I'm sure he would. But listen, are you gonna be naked in these pictures?" She sounded hopeful; I laughed and didn't answer, just put my laptop aside and reached for her.

The next day, because I didn't want Raquel to get a text from Andy and nothing from me, I sent her an email about the tango movie. Nothing too definite, only that I'd heard there were several interesting parts and would really like to see the script if those parts were still available. Then I put in some time in the studio and on the computer, because I needed to be in shape and prepared for the job I already had.

When I got to Andy's studio later that week, he was finishing up a session. I walked in to find Ray's sister Charlene and her husband Juan looking through the images on Andy's giant flatscreen. Andy glanced over at me and said, "Hi Lucas. This is what we're doing."

"Wow," I said, because the photo on-screen when I looked over was amazing. Juan was crouched on the floor, balanced on one foot and one shin, with one hand touching the floor and the other arm extended up, on the same angle as his back. He was looking up intently, his head in three-quarter profile. His waist-length black-and-silver hair was loose, half-covering his face and obscuring his bare body. The Pacific-Northwest-style full-sleeve tattoo on the extended arm was in sharp focus.

He glanced over at me. "I'm playing Wolf," he said, with a tiny smile, and I got it; the triangular shape looked like a wolf sitting down to howl. Andy had told me the title of the show was 'The Male Animal.' Based on this, Grace was going to like the pictures.

I went over and shook hands with everybody, leaning in to kiss Charlene's cheek. "How you doing, Charlene? You happy to be back in L.A.?"

"We're still adjusting," she said. "Thank goodness we can run back to the Peninsula for the summer. But Mom and Dad love having the kids here." I knew she and Juan had two kids now. I'd never gotten to know the family, but Ray had mentioned them enough times. One thing I did know was that Juan was a jeweler. I noticed the ring that Charlene was wearing. It was not an ordinary wedding ring. I was willing to bet Juan made it.

"I have a job for you, Juan," I said. "Grace and I are engaged."

"Are you? Congratulations. When is the wedding?"

"June. Soon as they cut me loose from this thing I'm working on in Las Vegas. Sorry, I don't want to barge in on your session." I gave Juan one of my business cards and went across the room to wait my turn while they focused back on the screen. After about ten minutes the tone of the murmured conversation changed.

Then I heard Charlene say, "Why aren't you in this show, Andy? You keep not putting yourself in."

"I'm everywhere," he said. "But the truth is I don't think of myself as a subject. And I'd have to use a mirror so I could see what the hell I was doing, and the remote shutter trigger, and then I'd have to touch up the images to take out the cord and it's all too much trouble."

Charlene laughed. "So many excuses. I think you should do it. We've got two kids, you know, I take a *lot* of pictures."

"And the truth is she wasn't expecting us to get done so fast," said Juan. "Sometimes we enjoy a child-free hour or three." Over in the corner, I couldn't help laughing. Juan looked over at me, clearly amused. "What animal is he, Lucas?"

"I'm not sure. Heard a rumor he can dance. Think we should see it?"

"What the *hell* is going on here?" Andy said. "Don't any of you have anywhere to be?"

"Grace told me to stay out for a while," I said, which was true. "She's editing an article and she says I'm distracting." Juan and Charlene both laughed at that.

141

"Fine, whatever." Andy got up and went into the studio's bathroom for a few minutes. When he came out he was wearing dance trunks, Dance Paws, and nothing else. I was impressed. He struck a pose. "Direct me!"

"Warm up," said Charlene, picking up the digital SLR he'd left on the desk. "Lucas, find him some music."

The whole thing was cracking me up, but I could tell from watching him, dutifully doing a little warm-up, that Andy still did really dance. So I went over to the sound system and snooped through his music library until I found what I was hoping to find, and turned it on.

Andy listened for a few seconds and then busted a gut laughing. "Seriously? 'Swan Lake?'"

"You ready there, Charlene?" I said.

"I'm on it," she said, smiling. I leaned against the counter and watched. Andy might have started out laughing but before long he was improvising something that looked a lot like real ballet to me. A few minutes in, he'd obviously decided to be serious about it, and started doing things that were slower, more extended. Charlene was firing away with the camera. I saw something that made me think, *that's it*, and Charlene also said, "That's it," but she kept shooting as long as Andy kept dancing.

Eventually he said, "Okay, the swan is dead," and subsided gracefully onto the floor. He rolled onto his back and lay there breathing hard. "Hecking heck, I haven't done anything like that for a little too long."

"Great flexibility," I said. "How old *are* you, anyway?"

Juan laughed again. Andy gave me a hateful look and said, "None of your business."

"Fifty-one," said Charlene. "I saw it on Wikipedia." I was impressed again.

"Gaahh." Andy sat up, got laboriously to his feet, and went to get dressed again. When he came out, Charlene handed him the camera.

"I think there's a few things you'll like," she said. "You don't have to show us, though."

"Well, why not?" he said. "Anybody want a drink besides me? It's five o'clock somewhere." Apparently we all agreed. He got a bottle of champagne out of the mini-fridge under the counter. I dug up my phone while he was pouring. Sent a quick text to Grace to give her an idea what was going on; I was surely going to be a lot later getting back than I'd thought.

We sat around looking at the pictures, drinking champagne, and generally having fun. We all agreed that one of the images needed to go in the show. In the picture, Andy was standing in profile to the camera, with his weight back on one foot, the back leg bent, and the other extended forward in what was called 'tendu.' He was bent forward from the hips with his back stretched down over that forward foot and both arms extended up behind him, just above the line of his back, with his palms up and fingers fanned out. It was a beautiful, and very swan-like, position. "Thanks for making me do that," he said. "I need to be reminded sometimes."

"It was great to see," I said. "Now I'll be less self-conscious about doing stuff for you."

"And on that note," Charlene said, "we'll get out of your hair. This was fun, Andy. Give us a buzz when the show goes up, right?"

"Right. Thanks, Juan. Take care of those kids." The three of them hugged and then Charlene and Juan left. Andy turned to me with a face that said 'your time has come,' and tipped his head toward the bathroom.

"Right," I said, and went to strip down to my trunks.

"What music do you want?" he asked when I came out.

"What animal am I?"

He tipped his head to one side, eyes narrowed as if he was just now thinking about this. Somehow I doubted that. "I see you as a mustang."

"Okay." I thought for a second. "Got any Nancy Sinatra?"

"Who do you think you're talking to?"

I was good and tired when I got home, in the dark, after six. The first glass of champagne had worn off while I was moving, but we'd had another while we reviewed the pictures. I hadn't had anything to eat since I left around noon, and I was sufficiently focused on getting inside and kissing Grace and fixing dinner that I didn't notice, at first, the car parked on the street in front of the house. It was only when I was closing the door that I thought, *huh.*

"Grace?" I called out as I went into the kitchen. "Andy worked me over, I'm starving. You ready to eat?" She didn't answer right away, so after I had a glass of water I went looking for her. There was only one place downstairs where she spent much alone time, so I went there first. "Grace? You around?"

When I stepped into the garden room, I saw her sitting next to someone, and started to smile. She looked really glad to see me. But she also looked tense, and nervous. So I focused on the other person there, and I know my face changed. He had his hand on her arm. Not simply resting there, but gripping it. When he saw where my eyes went he let go of her like he'd been scalded.

"Hi Lucas," said Grace. Her voice was a little thin. "This is Chris. The guy I was seeing last winter."

144

"Well Chris," I said, and my voice came out like I'd never heard it, "I think it's time for you to go." He stood up in a hurry, sidling past me without speaking. I followed him to the front door, down the driveway, and to his car. He wasn't a small guy, but he looked scared half to death, and I hoped he was. I was pleased to see a parking ticket under his windshield wiper. He picked it up, unlocked the car, and opened the door. Before he got in I said, "Don't come back here."

He shook his head. He didn't say anything. He got into the car, started it up, and drove away. I stood there for a few minutes, realizing I'd never felt so violent in my life, and doing some breathing to chill myself out. When I turned around Grace was standing in the doorway.

VIII - Grace
January 2018

Lucas walked back up the driveway to me and stopped at the bottom of the front steps. "Are you all right?" His voice was still a bit ... dark. I wondered if he realized it. He'd sounded truly dangerous a few minutes ago.

"I'm fine." He took two steps up and stopped again, putting his hands on my waist. I tipped my forehead down to his. "I was a little freaked out. Now I'm just really frigging *mad*." He huffed out a laugh. I stepped back and he followed me into the house.

"You know, when we started shooting the assault storyline, the production did this class on consent. A lot of people said, after that, they'd never even thought about it before. Ain't that a kick in the head?" His voice sounded normal now. "Can I kiss you?"

"Anytime, anyplace, anyhow." So he did, for a while. I felt a lot better after that. Still mad, though, and now plenty stirred up on top of that. "How hungry are you?"

"Not that hungry." He knew what I meant. We went upstairs, and took our clothes off, and for about a half hour he let me do anything I wanted with him. When I finally let him finish, and then collapsed, he said (after a few minutes to catch his breath), "Whew. What else makes you mad?" That made me laugh good and hard, and after that I really was hungry.

So we put ourselves back together and went downstairs, and dug through the fridge for whatever was fast and easy. We ate standing up, drinking wine poured from the already-open bottle that was on the counter. Lucas told me about his afternoon. I'd gotten my article done, but I wished I'd gone with him. "I can't wait to see the pictures. Is he going to send you the whole set?"

"Yeah. I'll be interested to see if you can pick out the one he liked the best for the show."

"You realize you're going to have a whole new fan base. Andy's got a pretty deep contact list." A lot of those contacts were in the gay community, which I didn't think would bother Lucas. He was pretty tight with the people in the Cabaret, not to mention his cast-mates on 'Behind the Strip.'

He may have guessed what I meant. "I love all my fans," he said, smiling. "Wherever they come from." He regarded me for a minute, and I knew he wanted to ask about the whole Chris thing.

"I would never have expected to be afraid of him," I said. "When he rang the doorbell and I saw who it was, I thought, oh, haven't seen him for a long time, wonder what's up, and opened the door."

"How did he know where you live?"

I knew it wasn't an accusation. Only a question. "He brought me home a few times."

"Was he here for a while?"

"Not long. Maybe fifteen minutes. He only put his hand on me right before you found us. It was like he didn't want me to answer you." I thought about that. "Did he really think you wouldn't come looking for me?"

Lucas' face said 'if he did, he's an idiot.' "What did he want?"

"I don't even know. I didn't get around to asking. He made some conversation about the classes he's handling this year. He's a teaching assistant, he's doing a doctoral program. I hadn't seen him or spoken to him since last May. What the flipping heck." I saw his eyes

147

flicker and knew he wanted to laugh at my adolescent swear substitutes. "Okay, what the fucking fuck." He laughed out loud. "I really love you. Thank you for scaring a year off the life of the creep I didn't know was a creep."

He leaned in and kissed me. "Maybe he's not really a creep. Maybe he had a moment of possessiveness, and forgot himself."

"That's a generous hypothesis." I was still mad.. "Especially considering you sounded like you wanted to tear his head off."

He moved in close, an arm around my waist. "It wasn't that he was touching you. It was that you were scared."

I put my head on his shoulder. "I know. Anyway, here's hoping he never forgets himself again. And also that I never hear from him again. I assure you, I won't be making contact."

"You should if you want to," he said, surprising me. "If you want to ask him what the hell he thought he was doing. I told him never to come here again, but if you see him on campus you might want to talk it out."

"On the theory that he's more likely to grasp what was wrong with what he did if we talk it out? Eh, it's a theory. Is that something they talked about in the class your production did?"

"Yeah." He hugged me. I leaned against that broad chest and thought *this is home*, and then I remembered he was leaving in a couple of days, and sighed. "What?"

"This whole long-distance engagement thing is a crock."

"I cannot disagree. But I've had quite a workout today, actually two workouts, and that was my third glass of wine. Wanna go watch TV for a while and zone out?"

"Yeah. There's this show I like, it's got this guy who looks like Elvis." He laughed, and we went down the hall to the den. He didn't cue up his own show, though. Instead he found something completely preposterous - I think it was something fast and furious - which served the purpose admirably.

The next day I was in my office (formerly my bedroom, and now still the guest room, but I needed a work space that wasn't in any of the social spaces) doing some reading for the imminent semester when I heard Lucas say "Whoa" from where he was working, down the hall in what used to be Mom's office.

"What?" I said without moving.

"Got an email from Raquel, with a script. It's that one Andy was talking about. Want to read it?"

"The email or the script?"

"Just the email for now." There was a smile in his voice. I loved the fact that I could tell. I got up to go down the hall. He leaned back in his task chair, looking up at me, and I thought *I can't believe this gorgeous man is mine*, and bent over to kiss him, stroking my hand down his perfect neck, before looking at the screen.

> Hi Lucas, As you undoubtedly know, Andy Martin pinged me about this project he and Victor Garcia have accepted without even asking me or Parker. Those guys are hard to keep up with. Anyway he thought you might be interested in seeing this script, or more accurately treatment. There was something about getting married, not wanting to go to Vancouver, boo hoo, whatever. And then I got your email.

I laughed. "Is this what she's always like?"

"Yeah, I love her. Andy's sharp, huh? We hardly said anything about the summer possibility." He had his hand on my ass. I pretended not to notice, kept reading.

> So here it is. Writer/director is Tanith Salazar, longtime voice artist for ABC/Disney, writer & director of 'What Went Down' 5.5 years ago here in L.A. (stage project), director of 'Green Darkness' (stage project) which you may have heard of since you did those other projects at Chrome also without asking me. What am I even here for. I talked to her and she says this project is going to be funded by a Kickstarter. It's going to pay union scale, so I'd be the last to say don't do it. Read it, see what you think, get back to me ASAP to let me know if you want to meet Salazar and read for a role.
> Cheers - Raquel

> p.s. VG is playing Gardel in the play-within-the-movie as well as the actor playing Gardel. Confused? Me too. AM part(s) not yet clarified. FML

"Union rates, shooting here in L.A., song and dance, movie? I feel like I hardly even need to read it," he said while I was still laughing.

"Read it anyway," I said. "It might suck." Though of course I doubted that, since Andy and Victor had both signed on, and they did not appear to be fools about their careers.

"Okay. Guess that's what I'm doing today. We can talk about it at dinner."

"Back to recycling and waste management on job sites for me." I kissed him again and went, reluctantly, back to my office.

By the time I knocked off work for the day, Lucas had read the script, and I'd heard tango music coming from the practice room. I could tell, at dinner, that he was fired up about it. "Was there a part you want?"

"Yeah. It's really twisty, every main part is basically two parts because it's this play inside the movie. The play part I kind of want is Francisco Fiorentino. Tanith put bio material in footnotes, the guy was a top tango singer after Carlos Gardel died. But we'll see if she likes how I read it."

"Did you already get back to Raquel?"

"Yeah. I'm hoping I can do the read tomorrow or Saturday." He had to go back to Las Vegas on Sunday. "I should listen to some more tango tonight."

"Have you ever seen 'The Tango Lesson'?"

"No, is it good?"

"It's great, it's about the artistic process as much as tango. Want to watch that first? Then I can go read some more while you study the music."

"Or we can watch it, then we can go fool around, and *then* you can go read."

That sounded like a good program to me, so that's what we did. We had definitely not yet reached the end of that phase, the phase of can't-keep-our-hands-off-each-other. Lucas had been working out daily, keeping fit for his part. He'd also been dancing quite a lot in the practice room, which was barely big enough for some of the stuff he did. We'd gone out to Dmitri's studio a few times for lessons, because Lucas had some upcoming scenes where they wanted swing dance. Anyway, long story short, the physical part of our relationship was not being neglected. I still thought his body was perfect. He seemed to like mine, too.

"I'll try to block out time for the ballroom club," I said after a while. "Even with the internship I should be able to. I need to work on rumba for the wedding."

"Yes you do," he said, smiling against my skin. We were lying there, not ready to go our separate ways. "Work on swing, too. I liked that song they had at the studio last time. 'Stop Drop and Roll.'"

"Or maybe I should ask Mateo to work on stuff with me. Probably more efficient. He could come over here if the times I can get to the studio don't work for him."

"Good idea." His hand was tracing patterns on my belly and breasts, straying tantalizingly to the tops of my thighs. I turned to him and kissed him again, pressing myself against him, and felt him respond. "If you stay there, we're not going to get much homework done."

"You started it," I pointed out, and hitched my knee up over his hip. He moved enough to bring us together again, hissing a little as he slid inside. "Mmm. I'm going to miss you."

"Grace." Only that. He rolled me to my back and went deep.

"God, Lucas." He kissed me. I wrapped my arm around his handsome head and moved with him. We did not do any of our homework.

The next morning after breakfast we got down to our business, because time was getting short. I stayed up in my office and Lucas went to the practice room. Mid-morning, he got a text from Raquel, which I knew because he came to find me, saying, "Reading at two in the Valley. I've gotta get ready. Do you want to come along?"

"Do you think they'd mind? I can bring stuff to read if they don't want me in the room, but, you know, every available minute with you is kind of what I want right now."

"Me too." He leaned down to kiss me. "Come with me. If they want you out of the room, they'll say so."

The reading was at a private house in Van Nuys. When we got there, we were greeted at the door by Mary Warner, the star of 'Green Darkness' and 'The Great Wave.' "You're here to read with Tanith?" she said, stepping back. "She's ready for you."

"Hi Mary," I said. I'd met her at Shall We Dance but hadn't realized this was her home. "Thanks for loaning the house. I guess it was kind of short notice to find another space."

"No worries. I'll be in my room if you need anything." She gave us both a beautiful smile and went out.

A small, pretty, dark woman came into the big living area from a back room. "Hi. I'm Tanith Salazar. You're obviously Lucas."

"This is my fiancée Grace Hart," said Lucas, setting down his guitar case. "She'll hang back if you prefer." We all shook hands.

"No issues with me. What do you know about Argentine tango?"

"A lot more than I knew a week ago," he said, and she laughed. "My friend Ray Daniels was in 'Gaucho' and I've seen that on video quite a few times."

"I'm sorry for your loss," Tanith said. "Alison and the others had good things to say about him."

He nodded an acknowledgement. "We also watched 'The Tango Lesson,' and I've been mainlining tango music. If you want me to sing, I worked on 'Mi Noche Triste' for a while this morning."

"I'd like to hear it. I've watched some of your show, so I know you can carry a tune. I know you can act, and I know you can dance. Have you read the treatment?"

"All of it."

"Great. This is about finding out if you get where I'm going, and if so, where we can put you. Okay?"

"Okay."

I hadn't ever been in the room for an audition before. It was not much like any of the (many) interviews I'd been to, but it wasn't too different from the project-related one-on-ones I'd done with advisors and experts. Both Lucas and Tanith focused in on the material and seemed to forget I was there. I sat across the room, quiet as I could possibly be, much too interested in what they were doing to pull out any of my reading.

And once again, Lucas impressed me. He'd learned that song by ear, and okay he was bilingual, but for him to have put it all together so fast made me think *wow*. I don't think it was simply my bias reading the same reaction into Tanith's face. He also didn't put any Elvis into it. I think he wanted to be clear that wasn't all he could do.

After that, she read a few scenes with him, which seemed to be for different characters. Some were clearly present-day, and some were obviously in the 1930s when most of the play-within-the-movie seemed to be set. How was that obvious? Well, whatever else she was, this Tanith was a good writer. It was the syntax and the choice of words, mostly.

It was a good hour before she sat back and stared at him for a long moment. He stared back at her with a little smile, and didn't say anything. I was dying to know what was about to happen. Finally she asked him, "Do you know Marco Hidalgo?"

"I know who he is."

"I'm his manager. He's got this script too. I want him in the Edmundo Rivero part. Which one do you want?"

Lucas said without hesitation, "Francisco Fiorentino."

"Great. I'll be in touch with your agent."

He smiled. "Can I ask you something?"

"Sure."

"Why are you handling casting yourself?"

"Because I can, and because I'm a control freak. Govern yourself accordingly."

He laughed, and stood up, holding out his hand for her to shake. Then he looked over at me. I got the message and stood up. "I'll look forward to hearing from Raquel."

"Stay out of trouble in Las Vegas," Tanith said, and sat back down with her tablet and her phone and her stack of notes, already absorbed in her work again. We let ourselves out.

When we got in the car Lucas leaned back against the headrest and blew out a breath. "That was intense."

"So they're not all like that?"

"Well, it's usually more than one person, and it's usually in a really neutral space, right? This time … you can tell who's in charge, that's for sure."

"I wonder if she does it that way as a strategy. It's got to be tough for a small, pretty woman to assert herself in a room with a bunch of other people."

"Huh. That could be it. Anyway, I guess we'd better get back so you can get some work done."

"Yeah." He started the car. I watched him drive for a few minutes, then turned to look out the window, smiling to myself. *He's going to be such a star.* "So tell me about tango."

VIII - Lucas
March 2018

I almost felt bad when Alison contacted me about working on a pro show that summer. There was no way I could, but I didn't think I'd miss it. With a wedding, the Underground Cabaret, New Zealand, and a movie lined up, it was looking like a banner year.

When I sent my regrets she sent back a text that said *There are so many of the usual suspects with conflicts, don't feel bad. I'd better get back to the drawing board.* I knew the tango movie was employing a lot of the people who'd participated in 'Face the Music.' Later on I heard through the grapevine that Alison had gone political, designing a show called 'Democracy.' I was hoping we'd at least get to go see it.

Grace and I talked or texted or emailed every day. Her schedule was jammed again, but with FaceTime we got some of that body-language feedback we'd both started to rely on. It made the separation less difficult. When 'Behind the Strip' suspended production for the spring break, I was in my car about a minute later.

The first thing I did after getting home was kiss Grace (a lot) and take her to bed. The next day I went out to Santa Monica to check in with Juan about her wedding ring. I'd sent him her ring size and my notion for a design to be cast in gold, and he'd sent me back a sketch that I thought was great. It was based on the Rialto bridge in Venice. I'd been in the city once and seen it. I knew she would recognize it. Grace's hands were delicate, so I'd been a little worried that the design might be too bulky, but Juan came through for me. The bridge's open arch would fit around a gemstone. He told me the size he needed and sent me on my way.

When I asked Grace if she wanted a diamond she said no. I'll admit, I was stumped; I didn't know much about jewelry. So I called Julia. "What do you think?" I asked. "Can you give me any hints? She doesn't wear any jewelry most of the time."

"Well," Julia said, "she's always liked opals."

"Thank you. I will now go and Google those because I barely know what one looks like."

She laughed. "I expect Juan has a few on hand. But yes, do a little research, because you will have other occasions to buy jewelry."

"Oh I will, huh? Good to know." I waited a second, then added, "What would those be?" because I thought it would make her laugh, and it did. "You doing okay up there in snow country?"

"I'm doing well, Lucas, thanks. Have you got any idea when I need to get myself to L.A.?"

I told her when the wedding was going to be. "So you're the first to know that we actually have a plan. Take care of yourself."

"You too. Take care of my girl."

"You know I will." After we disconnected I got online and learned a little bit, and then sent a text to Juan, and he got right back to me to confirm he had an opal that would fit the ring. So with that taken care of, I got on the phone with Rory.

We hadn't done more than send a few idea videos back and forth. This was our first chance to get in a room together and start really working on 'Hotel California.' I gave her Grace's schedule and she said, "I'll come over there tomorrow after she leaves for campus. We can work in your practice room at first. If it turns out to be too small, we can take it over to Dmitri's, right?"

"Right." I was all set up with music, coffee, and towels when she got there, but the first thing she said wasn't about the dance.

"So about this wedding." Rory looked stern, or as stern as someone can who is five foot one and has a face like a kitten's.

"Uh, yeah. Am I in trouble?"

"Who's doing it, where are you doing it, and when are you doing it?"

Oh, I thought, and smiled. "You are, in your yard, after dress rehearsal for 'On the Edge.' If that works." Grace and I had talked about it and agreed on this basic plan. I knew Rory was ordained by the Universal Life Church and had done weddings for at least three other couples associated with the Underground Cabaret. "Let me know what you need for the budget. I've been saving for a while."

"DJ and dance floor?"

"Yes please."

"Okee dokee. I'll have some numbers for you shortly. Now let's get to work."

By the time Grace got home I was flat out on the floor in the den, having downed a liter of water and a couple of Advil. She called from the front of the house, "Lucas? Honey, are you around?"

"I'm in the den," I called back. "I can't move." I heard her laughing as she came down the hall toward me. Playing it up a little, I turned my head to watch her feet approach, then looked up, going for 100% Pitiful.

Her expression was half sympathy and half laughter. "Wow. You look a little bit broken."

"I am. Can we order pizza tonight?"

"Absolutely."

"How was your day?"

"Busy. Fun. I guess yours was too."

"Yeah, it was fun, but I'm sure glad you and I got some quality time last night. And this morning."

"Especially this morning." She knelt down on the floor beside me and kissed me. I put a hand up and touched her beautiful face. "But I guess that means you're no good to me tonight."

"Well, I might revive a little after some pizza." She kissed me again, running a hand down my body. "Or maybe even before some pizza." She laughed and got to her feet.

"I'm hungry myself. I'll order, and open a bottle. If you're still awake thirty minutes after we eat, we'll see if you're capable of getting up the stairs. If not, I'll drag you onto the couch. Because the floor in here is not comfortable."

"No it isn't." This we knew from experience. "You know, this could make a good story someday. How I spent the afternoon with another woman and then had to spend the night on the couch."

"Yeah, and let's not forget that other woman is ten years older than you and presumably walked out of here under her own power. So how'd it go?"

I was laughing under my breath, figuring she would get Rory's side of the story before long. There had been equal-opportunity pain while we traded jazz stuff and hip-hop. "Great. I think I need food before I'll be able to remember specifics."

"Jeez, all right already. You stay there and rest." She got down to my level again, though, and laid her hand on my face, stroking down over my jaw and neck. Then her thumb swept over my mouth right before she kissed me again.

I ran a hand up her arm, across her shoulder, and into her still-short hair. "I love you."

"I love you too. Let me go get dinner rolling." She stood up again, and this time she actually left the room. I lay still, laughing to myself again because the one part of me that wasn't completely exhausted was wishing I could have moved fast enough to make her forget about food, floor or no floor. Then I rolled over and basically crawled to the couch. *Good thing this isn't the last day of my break*, I thought.

I did fall asleep on the couch after we ate, but managed to get myself up the stairs in the morning, not long before Grace's alarm was set to go off. "Hey," she said drowsily when I slid into bed beside her. She wrapped an arm around me and worked a leg in between mine. I kissed her throat, her face, and her mouth. "You seem to be recovered." She sounded more awake. Her hand went down my body. "Definitely recovered." I smiled against her skin and kissed her some more, loving the feel of her hand on me, and returning the favor until she made an impatient sound. She pushed me over and got on top, sliding down to take me in. She lay flat against me, hardly moving, with my hands roaming over her body, kissing me until those small movements suddenly became urgent and she rose up to finish us both.

"Holy wow," I said after a minute, when she was flat on her back beside me.

The alarm went off. She flung out a hand to silence it. "Wow is right," she said. "You know, I am reasonably certain that nobody I will see today has started the day off better than that." I laughed. She patted me randomly, and got out of bed. I meant to watch her walk across the room, but I fell asleep again.

161

I met up with Rory several more times during the break, but we'd done most of the vocabulary exchange that first day, and I didn't wreck myself again. Even a lifts session with Mike at Dmitri's studio wasn't too bad. Of course, the training I was doing in Las Vegas hadn't exactly gotten less strenuous. It was still nice to confirm that I could dance at pretty much the same level as I had ten years ago.

The third thirteen-episode run of 'Behind the Strip' was going to be released at the end of March, right before I went back to Vegas. The producers had done an edit of 'Today, Tomorrow and Forever,' mixing bits of all five versions we'd taped with pieces of Stephanie's scenes, for release as a video single. I'd brought a watermarked advance copy to show Grace. Kelly was going to have another video released too; social media for the show had made her a star on the circus-arts side. The other video planned for this season was a big production number of 'Gimme Shelter,' with Derek and Nancy featured on the music side. Head writer Kathy had told me, kind of hush-hush, that the show was going to promote the Panama episode for an Emmy nomination. We were hoping for at least one for our choreographer, too. It was an energizing place to be in, going back to work.

Meanwhile, Grace was in the homestretch for her degree. Jerry Weiss had already made her that offer, and it was a good one. We were talking about all six of her offers a couple days before I had to leave. "So you're still leaning toward Mr. Weiss, right?" I said.

"I am," she said, fiddling with her wine glass, "but I'm thinking of asking for something kind of big."

"More money? Or to work from Las Vegas?" I was half-joking, but she looked up at me and I could see in her face that I'd guessed right. I know I sounded hopeful when I said, "Really? Do you think he would go for it?"

"The two cities are not unmanageably far apart. And the vast majority of our work is done in our offices, not on job sites. I was thinking of suggesting half here, half there. Like, an alternating-weeks schedule. It wouldn't work for a lot of people because of the expenses, but since we already have a house here," she shrugged. Took a drink of her wine and set down the glass, leaning back, but leaving her hand on the table. I reached out for it and she wrapped her fingers around mine. "Of course this presupposes that your series is going to be back in production. I can't imagine they'll drop it. It's so good."

"Well, quality doesn't necessarily pay the bills. But it's buzzy, and it sure seems like it's making money." Raquel had found out, and passed on, that the show had been paid big bucks for product placement, and ad sales were strong. The cast album released in September was doing well, too, with a boost from its Grammy nomination. "In case you're wondering," I said, "I'd really love it if that worked out. I mean, if I go back to work on 'Strip,' if you could be with me at least half the time, that would be so great. I love being with you. I love you."

"I love you too." She leaned over and kissed me. "Okay, I'm going to ask for that. I'll let him know that the ask is contingent on your work. Or should I? For all I know, he knows a guy who can shut down your show."

I laughed. "Yeah, he knows a guy." I'd met Mr. Weiss when I stopped by the office to take Grace to lunch. He reminded me of Peter Falk in 'The Princess Bride.' He didn't seem like the kind of guy who'd fuck you over for his own convenience. So she talked to him the next day, and sent me a text that was only a thumbs-up. The feeling of relief was so strong, it was almost like being high. I sent back all the happy emojis and she answered with *LOL XOX.* Things between us were so easy that remembering we'd only been physically together for, basically, three months out of the thirty we'd known each other always tripped me. To know that if I went back to Las Vegas at the end of the summer I wouldn't be without her for weeks (or months) at a stretch was life-giving.

We met up at Andy's studio at the end of her day for a preview of his show. With some screwy scheduling for 'L.A. Vice' looming, he hadn't been able to promise Grace an advance look at all the images from the session. Since he was going to give us a disc with all of them, she had put on a saintly-patience act and returned her attention to her work. She was kind of buzzing when she got there, though.

"Do I want to see the full session first, or do I want to see what you've hung?" she asked Andy as soon as he opened the door.

"Oh, look at what's up first," he said. "It's a small show." The studio was basically one large high-ceilinged room, with a bathroom and kitchenette lined up on one short wall where the stairs came up, and three windows on one of the long walls. Looking at how he'd used the space, I thought *he planned ahead for this*, because he could fit framed prints on the window wall as well as on its opposite and the end wall. He had a total of twenty-four prints. "I had this same number in my very first show," he said nostalgically. "It seems like a long time ago."

The prints were all black and white, with white mats and thin black frames. Each image was of a different man. I shouldn't have been surprised by how many of them I knew. Obviously I knew Juan, and Andy himself, and then there was me. But almost all the male dancers I'd met on the shows at Chrome were on the walls, including Mike, doing one of his incredible things.

164

"Oh honey. You so belong here," Grace said, as if she'd read my mind. She'd gone directly to the picture of me. "How do you even *do* that?"

"Practice," I said, going over to her and wrapping an arm around her waist. "And not minding when you crash." The image Andy had chosen was of a b-boy trick called a butterfly twist. It was a fun one to do, once you got it.

"Are you doing a book this time?" Grace asked Andy. "I can imagine what else you got with all these guys. I mean, holy moly. This is a bunch of good-looking guys. Present company included."

He looked amused. "Thanks. There might be a book. I probably won't have time to even start on it till our winter break, thanks to this movie. So Lucas, I heard you'll be joining us on that project."

"Yeah, looking forward to it. Which of the play parts are you doing? Tanith didn't tell me."

"Alfredo Le Pera. The lyricist guy. So I also die in the plane crash, which seems so tragically romantic."

Grace laughed. "You're so nuts. But that isn't a singing part, is it?"

"Tanith's going to throw me a bone in the modern-day section. Also, I get to manage the chorus boys. Basically, the whole thing is about the chorus boys, if you ask me." He went over to the kitchenette and opened the mini-fridge, raising his eyebrows. "We could have a little something while you look at the session, unless you want to take it straight home."

"I wouldn't mind," I said. "I think we have something to celebrate."

"Yes we do," said Grace. So Andy poured some champagne (he must have always kept some in there) and we sat down to go through the photos. When we got home, Grace let me know how much she liked them.

And then I had to go back to work.

IX - Grace
June 2018

Dad approved of my deal with Jerry Weiss. Mom approved of me working out a way to spend more time with Lucas. And the world in general approved of 'Behind the Strip,' at least to the extent of deals getting made for another 26-episode order, which the cast heard about before production wrapped on the fourth run.

I graduated magna cum laude and went straight to work full-time with Weiss & Associates. Lucas moved back home as soon as the production cut him loose. He went straight into the studio to work with Rory on their number for the Underground Cabaret. He also began training with the Argentine tango dance team for 'The Ghost of Carlos Gardel,' and started putting together the guitar-and-vocal numbers he'd be doing in the film.

Somewhere in there, we went to Beverly Hills City Hall and got our marriage license. Wow was that an unreal day. Once everything was signed and I secured the document in my bag, we went outside and stood in the garden holding each other and giggling. It was such a sweet, ridiculous moment. All I wanted to do was go home with him and celebrate. But he had a meeting with Raquel, and I had to go back to the office. So, like grown-ups, we kissed and said "See you tonight," and went our separate ways.

Jerry wasn't assigning me a lot of stuff right up front. He told me that it would start to hit after we got back from New Zealand. I spent a lot of my work time reviewing the company's previous work and reading up on current projects. I would be working on a team focusing on urban planning and redevelopment, with occasional contributions to Jerry's residential team. I already knew that they'd worked on Andy and Victor's duplex; it was fun to get my hands on those plans.

It was almost funny how normal things felt at home. So much was changing, in such meaningful ways. But my routine really wasn't going to change until I started going back and forth to Las Vegas: I was used to doing my thing (research and other work) at home while the other main person was out and about all the time doing artsy stuff. Lucas asked me once if I minded his crazy schedule, and the fact that there was usually music playing. I told him, "That's what home was always like, to me." For some reason that got me a big hug and a kiss.

But later I realized there was more I could say about it. "It's like this," I said. My head was on his shoulder, my arm draped across his bare chest. "What you do is so different from what I do. Hearing about it, or seeing your work, is inspiring. It's exciting. It's refreshing. I come home from however many hours of staring at a screen - you know I like what I do, but still - and here you are, so active and creative. Last week, when you were in the practice room? And I went back there and the music was great, and you started dancing with me? I love that."

He kissed me. "Sharysse got tired of it. To her, after a while, it was just commotion. Nothing but noise."

"Did she want you to do something else instead?"

"I don't know if it was so much that. But when she got home, she wanted me there for her, but she wanted it quiet. She wanted a routine. And, well." He stopped.

I thought, *there's something there*. "What?"

He answered slowly. "She wanted to have a baby. Well, it figures, right? The minute we were done, she got pregnant."

"What did you guys use?"

"Diaphragm and condoms. We were careful."

"We haven't really talked about ... that, have we?"

"It's not too late." He turned toward me, shifting his weight to his side. "Do you want to have kids?"

"I'm not sure," I said. "I've been so focused on school, and for the next few years at least I want to focus on my career. I want to be a partner in the firm by the time I'm thirty. In this firm, or if that isn't happening, I'll need to find a new position." I stopped talking, and only then realized that I'd changed the subject.

He changed it back. "But you've thought about it, right?" His tone was very neutral, uninflected, but I was feeling a little defensive. *Why*, I thought, because one thing I could count on with Lucas: he was never on the attack with me.

"Give me a minute," I said. "I've got some stuff working and I don't know where it's coming from. Can I just kiss you for a while?" He laughed. "Not stalling, I promise. I kind of like kissing you."

"I like kissing you, too." He did some of that, and as usual it was great, but when I would have taken it farther (again) he backed off, even though I could tell part of him was totally in favor. "Come on, Grace. Whatever it is, we can figure it out."

So I blurted out the first thing in my head. "I feel like I'm *supposed* to want kids."

After a second, he said, "Okay?" It was like, I'm following, not quite there.

I patted his chest. "I think I'm reacting to that instead of really thinking it through. I'll tell you one thing, though, I'm not used to kids. I don't know how to act with kids. So this idea that I should want them, I guess, puts my back up. But *you* don't want kids, do you?"

"I didn't. I don't." I appreciated that he didn't try to soften it. He went on, "I had that experience of having to be responsible when I was maybe a little too young, and I saw an awful lot of my classmates and crewmates get … not dragged down, exactly, but maybe I'd say pinned down. By that kind of responsibility. I also knew guys who walked away from it, and a couple of them never seemed to care, but a couple of them never got over it. It was like, leaving a woman and a child kind of broke them. Those guys have never had a solid relationship since."

"And other guys had to make compromises, didn't they. In order to be responsible. Had to give up opportunities." I wasn't really asking a question, but he nodded. "I think that's why I put it in a box. To me it wasn't an option to want kids because, based on everything I saw around me, having kids would pretty much stop my career for ten years. And that hasn't changed simply because I now have this awesome gorgeous hunk of prime genetic material next to me."

He laughed. "Well, things do change. Our feelings might change. Ten years from now we might be in a different place and we might look at it a different way."

I still didn't know what to tell him. There was one thing I wasn't sure he'd considered, but that was always in the back of my mind. Just this tiny anxiety, ever since we'd both gotten the all-clear and stopped using condoms, because up to now I'd always been a two-method girl. "What about contraceptive failure? The Pill is good, but it's not a hundred percent. What would you want to do?"

He blew out a breath and rolled onto his back again. After a moment he said, "That's a tough one. It's a lot easier to say I don't want kids when nobody's pregnant, you know what I mean?"

"Yeah, exactly. I wouldn't set out to get pregnant, but if it happened because we lost a roll of the dice, I'm not sure I could, you know. I love you so much. I'd be terrified and pissed off and losing my mind, but I'm not sure I could intentionally destroy anything we made together. Even though we didn't mean to, even though we didn't want to. Even though I know perfectly well that, scientifically speaking, it's only the *possibility* that we'd be saying goodbye to."

He turned his head, gazing at me with those dark serious eyes, and it seemed like we'd come to the heart of it. "That's kind of where I'm at. Because I love you so much, too. I could never want to hurt you, or any part of you, or anything you made." He rolled back over and hugged me and kissed me, possibly because he'd seen the tears in my eyes. "I could get a vasectomy."

"Whoa. Where'd that come from?" It was so far beyond anything I'd ever considered asking him to do that I hadn't thought of it even now.

"I right this second remembered this time during prep for 'The Great Wave.' Mike was walking a little funny. I asked him what was up, and that's what he did. Said he'd gone to the clinic and put some away just in case, but Paula was basically No Way No How, and they were planning this vacation to Argentina. With all the travel and some wine expectations, they didn't like their odds." I laughed. Lucas smiled. "Anyway, maybe that's a strategy? 'Cause then if we ever changed our minds, there'd still be a way." He kissed me again. "If that's what you want to do, I'll do it."

"I really love you." I tucked my head into the curve of his neck for a minute. "If you'd really do that … honestly, it would take such a load off. Knowing that if someday we decide yes, we can, but until and unless, we don't have to, like, *worry*."

"Have you been worried? I'm sorry."

"The odds were in our favor," I pointed out. "But yeah. I mean, even if both of us were all whatever happens, happens, that would be a major derailment."

"I love you. I'll take care of it." Then we finally stopped talking and got back to rolling the dice.

I didn't have to ask Lucas *when* he took care of it. It was kind of a giveaway when I got home one day and instead of him being in the practice room, he was sitting in the den watching TV with a cold pack you-know-where. The after-care instructions put a crimp in our style for a few days, and the clinic was really clear about Keep Using Your Method for a couple of months until follow-up tests could be done. I wouldn't have thought it was possible for me to love him more, but the fact that he'd do that for me was like a warm drink on a cold day.

Things were really busy there for a while. Dress rehearsal for 'On the Edge' was the morning of June sixteenth, our wedding was that afternoon, and the show was set for the next two nights. We'd be leaving for New Zealand the following Thursday. Mom flew in on the tenth to spend a couple of weeks with us in L.A. She insisted on sleeping in the guest room, which was *so weird*, and spent most of the daytime hours catching up with friends.

Dad came over for dinner a couple of times, which was also so weird. I mean, there was a tinge of that meeting-the-parents thing, because we hadn't done it like that with the four of us before, but there was also a tinge of wrongness in being the hosts in the house that used to be theirs. To their credit, Mom and Dad were both perfect guests and neither of them even made any jokes about being kicked out of the nest they'd built.

Luisa and Cesar came over for one of those dinners, too. Lucas told me later that they both liked the house and were excited for the wedding. I knew that last part; they weren't shy about saying so. It was sweet, and reassuring. There was a lot of general chatter about Lucas' series and all the awards buzz it was starting to get. We got into talking shop for a while. Mom was enjoying her job, Dad had made a couple of big deals, and Luisa had been promoted to nurse manager at the hospital where she worked. And, since Cesar worked on the Metro, I was able to have an interesting conversation with him about public transit.

Yet another thing I had to take care of, and had kind of left till the last minute, was What To Wear. Obviously a backyard wedding is a little more casual, but Lucas and Rory were handling the details and I really didn't know which way they were going. When I asked Lucas what he was wearing he gave me one of those sideways looks and smiled, and said, "A tuxedo." I didn't even know he had one. When I said so, he said, "Well, it's new," and he was obviously so close to laughing that I got as irritated with him as I had ever been. And of course, I was irritated because I didn't want to admit that I hadn't planned ahead. It was so unlike me.

Finally, with only days to go, I begged Mom for help, and *she* laughed at me too. Only openly. "Really?" she said, still laughing.

"I've been BUSY," I said, exasperated.

"You know one of the best designers in Los Angeles, he's a personal friend, and you haven't done this. I can't believe you, Gracie Hart." She got her phone out and called Kenji Matsumoto. "Hi Kenji, do you have a minute? Thanks. Yes, I'm well. Looking forward to seeing you this weekend. And actually I'm calling about that. Yes. My darling daughter seems to have … not secured a wedding dress." She laughed. "Oh yes, she really wants to get married." I rolled my eyes. "I remember, Michelle told me she did the same thing. Oh really? They're close to the same size, aren't they? She wouldn't mind? When could we come over?" Mom looked at me and said, "You need to take tomorrow morning off work," and I shrugged and nodded, sending a text to Jerry immediately, because the context clues were telling me what was about to happen. Mom said to Kenji, "We'll be there at nine-thirty. Thanks, Kenji. Say hi and thanks to Michelle, too."

After she disconnected, I said, "So am I trying on Michelle's wedding dress?"

"You'll love it," Mom said. "So will Lucas."

Once I saw it, I had to agree. I was an inch taller than Michelle, but it was all in my legs; the waist and bust fit perfectly. The style was Fifties glamour, tea-length, in a pale oyster grey with an iridescent pink sheen to it. The dress had a portrait neckline with a spread-collar back and was decorated with pearls and rhinestones. Mom had told me to bring the silk slip, so I had, and I have to say I looked as close to 'movie star' as I was ever going to. When I thought of how Lucas was undoubtedly going to look (that is, like a movie star), I said, "You know, this is why I didn't try to find a dress. Because nothing but this would have been so perfect." Mom patted my back. Kenji only smiled. "It's a damn shame I can't wear Michelle's shoes, too."

Mom laughed at that, and went to get her tote bag. She pulled out my high-heeled saddle shoes. They were turquoise and white, not the right color combo at all, but she handed them to Kenji. He said, "I'll take care of it," and I knew they would be perfect too.

The dance I was doing with Rory had come together really well. During our practices she gave me a little of her history, how she started out in dance and gymnastics, but after coming to L.A. had gotten hooked into the group of burlesque artists who'd started the Underground Cabaret. I found some of her strip routines online, and the jazz things she'd started to do in the last couple of years. Plus, of course, I'd seen her 'Human Nature' number, with Mike and two other girls. The woman had a twisted imagination and a great sense of humor. Once we worked in some hip-hop and a few of my b-boy tricks (Rory learned a couple herself), it was the right combination for 'Hotel California.'

At dress rehearsal we got a look at the other numbers in the show. Not all were explicitly about California. Mike and Paula were opening the show, dancing to Queen's 'Leaving Home Ain't Easy,' which would speak to all the audience members who'd come to the state from somewhere else. Rory and I opened Act Two. Cabaret regulars Vince and Kelli closed the show with an Argentine tango set to Queen Latifah's cover of 'California Dreaming.' I'd met them both the previous year on 'Face the Music.' Vince was Michelle's new ballroom partner, but he also danced with his wife in the Cabaret and in tango competitions.

I knew Grace wasn't interested in being a performer, but at least she liked dancing with me. She'd put in a lot of work with me on our wedding dance. I wasn't nervous about the dance itself. Dancing to my own vocal recording, on the other hand, had me a little tweaked. Maybe I thought it was kind of conceited. But when I'd suggested using the Elvis/Ann-Margret recording, Grace had given me a flat No. So mine it would be; I'd been given a disc, back in December, by a certain soft-hearted director.

I hadn't yet told Grace about an email I'd gotten from Tanith. It wasn't about the upcoming movie shoot, or any of the preliminary rehearsal we were doing. I was going to show it to Grace after the wedding, after 'On the Edge,' when we both had fewer things to think about. The long flight to New Zealand seemed like the perfect time.

Dress rehearsal wrapped up right on schedule, with very few notes from the director or stage manager. I guess so many of the Cabaret performers had been participating for so long, everyone literally had their act together. It worked out great for me, anyway, because I was able to get out of the nightclub, run home to get showered and dressed, and get over to Rory and Dana's house before Grace and Julia got back from the salon.

"I'm going glam," she'd warned me. "You've never seen me like this before. Mom is going to make you cover your eyes or something when we get there so I can get into the cottage to get dressed."

"Seriously? We're doing the don't see the bride before the wedding thing?" I thought it was cute, actually. "Okay, have her text me. I'll go around the back till I get the ready signal." I was done going through the checklist with Rory, done inspecting the arrangements (which looked great), and done checking in with our DJ, Cabaret producer Danny, by the time I got Julia's text. Andy was already roaming around, taking candid pictures for what he'd described to me as 'coverage,' and it was seriously surreal having a TV star taking pictures for my wedding. My whole family was already there, as were Mike and Paula and a bunch of the Cabaret gang. I grabbed Mike and made him come around the back of the cottage with me, telling him I'd been instructed to make myself scarce.

"Mateo did the don't see the bride thing too," Mike said. "Last year when he and Sam got married. Sam had to hang back for a while, but it was all worth it." He got his phone out and showed me a picture of Mateo, who'd dressed in full kimono for the ceremony.

The makeup, costume and wig were amazing. Mateo had one of those Filipino faces that is beautiful on a woman but a knockout on a man. "Wow. I'll bet that took a little time."

"Right up to the minute. You all set?"

"I am so ready for this."

He smiled in a way that said he knew what I meant. "Did Kenji make that tux for you?"

"No, actually, it's from the show. One of the last things we were doing was, we had this big mambo production number to 'Surrender,' and they wanted to cut in me singing the backing track. They're going to drop another video single. So anyway, they gave me this for taping the vocal. I wasn't really supposed to take it off the soundstage." I'm sure he could tell I wasn't too worried about getting in trouble.

"Damn, I was hoping I could get one. Paula likes it."

I liked it, too. It was made with this stuff that had a little shine to it, like gunmetal. "I'll bet he can make one for you. I can find out where they got the fabric and stuff." You would think we were fashion hounds, instead of a couple guys trying to make their women happy, right?

"I'll ask him to use it for inspiration. We wouldn't want to be too matchy-matchy." He was grinning for real now, he must have had the same thought.

"Yeah, people would think we were a couple. Not that there's anything wrong with that." He laughed while I looked him over; he was wearing a white suit, one I'd seen him in before. "Isn't that from your 'Dancing in the Dark' thing?"

"Uh-huh. Paula likes this, too." We both cracked up.

And then, finally, my phone vibrated again. Mike saw me focus and didn't even ask, just walked with me around the cottage. The chairs set up on and around the dance floor were nearly all occupied. Rory was standing at the front, on a riser (hey, she's short); Danny was set up and spinning Sinatra over to one side. I didn't see Andy, but I'm sure he was around there somewhere. Rory caught my eye and waved, so I shook hands with Mike and then went to join her. "You ready for this?" she said.

"Am I ever."

"Good boy." I'm guessing she was getting signals too. She made a sign to Danny, and he faded out the track in play and started playing 'Can't Help Falling in Love with You.' I don't know how he did it but it was *my* version, which wasn't on the cast album. I glanced over at him and he gave me a thumbs-up. Then there was a little bit of a commotion. I turned my head, and there was Grace at the back of the seating area, starting down the aisle with her dad. God only knows what my face looked like when I saw her. Well, I know now, because of course Andy caught it.

She looked ... stunning. The dress was gorgeous, and I could tell her shoes were sparkly. But her hair had been done in a very Fifties style of short curls, and her eyes were made up like Elizabeth Taylor's, and even though she never wore lipstick in real life, her mouth was done in a rosy red. I would have walked out to meet her if Rory hadn't gotten me by the arm. "You stay here," she warned, very low. When I met her eyes she was clearly about to bust up laughing. I smiled then, and looked back at Grace, and she smiled too. Then she was there beside me. Her dad kissed her cheek and stepped back to stand beside Julia, in the front row with my mom and dad.

"Grace," I said softly.

"Lucas."

"You look beautiful."

"So do you." She grinned at me, and I wanted to kiss her, but Rory still had a hold of me.

"I swear, you guys," she hissed. "Just wait a goddamn minute." She raised her voice then. "Dearly beloved!" And she went into the ceremony. I know I listened, because I didn't miss any of my responses. When she asked for the ring, I pulled it out of my pocket. Grace surprised me then, because she gave me a ring too. It was heavy gold, with a suggestion of architecture in the design; it suited my big rough hand perfectly. Then I thought it was about time that Rory gave me permission to kiss my wife, but she didn't. She said to Grace, "So did you get the whole old, new, borrowed, blue thing going?"

Grace said, "Old slip, new ring, borrowed dress, blue thong," and I thought I was about to pass out. Rory was cracking up, as were the people in the front row.

Finally, *finally*, Rory said, "Hey Lucas, how about you kiss the bride?" I slid my arm around Grace's waist and drew her close. She laid a hand on my face, her gaze meeting mine for a long sweet moment before I kissed her. I had enough sense to think *she kept the downstage side open*, and it made me laugh. In a second, she was laughing too.

"Good stagecraft there, Mrs. Gutierrez," I said. The guests were applauding. I kissed Grace again. "Are you sure you don't want to be in show business?"

"I want to be in *your* business right now," she said. Rory laughed out loud and stepped off the riser.

"There you go, everybody. Mr. and Mrs. Lucas Gutierrez. Somebody pop the champagne!" Somebody did. Rory patted my back, then leaned in (and stretched up) to kiss Grace's cheek. A moment later, our parents were there with us and a whole lot of hugging was going on.

"Can you even believe how good-looking he is?" Grace was saying to her mother. "I mean *really*." Julia was laughing. So was my mom. "Where did you get this?" Grace was fingering the tuxedo. "Did Kenji make it?"

"No, I stole it from 'Behind the Strip.'"

"Oh shit, really?" She looked delighted. "Well, it's awesome."

"That dress is pretty special, too."

"Kenji made it for Michelle when they got married. Good thing we're almost the same size. I completely failed on the planning-ahead thing. Except for getting your ring."

"It's beautiful, I love it. And the dress is perfect on you," I said. Someone was bringing champagne around. We both had glasses in our hands without quite knowing how they got there. Somehow we started to circulate. We weren't far from each other at any time, and I was always acutely aware of Grace's location. I thought she must have been feeling the same, because every time I looked for her she was already looking back at me. *This is torture*, I thought, loving it.

After a half hour or so, I realized that the dance floor had been cleared. Mike came up to me and said, "Time for act two," and took the empty glass out of my hand. Paula brought Grace over. Whatever Danny was playing faded out. A second later, my 'Today, Tomorrow and Forever' started. I took Grace into dance hold.

The song was so quiet that it took about thirty seconds for everyone to realize what was happening. I'd thought that might happen, so the first part of the dance was super simple. Which worked out perfectly, because it settled me down. Grace too, apparently, because she kind of melted against me, and when I started leading our choreography she went into it looking relaxed.

I'd gotten help from a lot of people to put that dance together, but in the moment it felt like I was making it up as we went along. We'd tried a few things for a big finish. You know how a lot of wedding dances end with some kind of a drop. Well, we had to be different, so we went with a lift. A simple one, just me holding Grace up with her hands on my shoulders, but we got tricky with the dismount. Instead of setting her straight down, I turned her a bit so one of her arms could go around my neck as I lowered her, and scooped up her legs to turn it into an over-the-threshold thing. Then I went down on one knee, still cradling her in my arms, and kissed her as the music ended. She tipped her forehead against mine, giggling, as the applause started. "So let me ask you again about show business," I said, and she laughed out loud. "Because I really like dancing with you."

"We'll see," she said. "Maybe when we're not so busy with other stuff."

"All right then." I let her get her feet under her, and we both straightened up, and then there were more hugs and lots of congratulations. Andy set us up for some regulation photos, food was served, champagne kept

181

flowing, people were dancing. Before we knew it the sun had set and people were starting to drift away.

Grace found me again and took my hand. "Is it time to go home?"

"We're not going home." I walked her around for a round of thanks and goodbyes, then picked up her gear from the chair where Julia had put it for me. "We're going to be private tonight."

"Oh! Where are we going?"

"Wait and see." She didn't argue, simply came with me and waited while the valet brought my car around. We didn't talk much then, or in the car. We were both a little tired; getting married isn't exactly hard work, but it's kind of a performance, and the adrenaline had been pumping all day. When I pulled in to the Four Seasons not much later, Grace made a sound of contented comprehension. Another valet took the car, we went inside, I got our room key, and we went upstairs.

"Oh Lucas," she said when we stepped into the room. I'd arranged for flowers, and a fancy dessert. Instead of more champagne there was a Thermos pot of decaf with cream. An overnight bag had been delivered earlier. "You thought of everything."

"I tried. Your mom helped." She turned around and hugged me. It felt so good to hold her. I hoped I would never get used to it. She pressed her lips to my neck and a moment later we were kissing.

We took our time getting undressed, being careful with our borrowed clothes, and we took our time in bed, leaving the lamps on because it seemed we both couldn't get enough of looking at each other. There was no hurry. We knew how to please each other. The fact that we were finally husband and wife made it all the sweeter. For the record, the thong was sky-blue silk and lace.

182

"Damn, girl," I said after a while. "Look at those legs. Gotta say, if you do like your mom and decide to be a dancer later on, I am so down for that."

She laughed. "I know you are. Right now everything I'm doing at work is exciting and new, it's taking up most of my brain space. Someday it might be oh, that again, ho hum. Then I'll need a little excitement."

"I will do what I can to provide it," I promised.

"I know you will." She stretched, and sat up to untangle the sheets. "I should take off this makeup." The lipstick was long gone, but the eye makeup still looked great. Slightly smudged, but in a very sexy way.

"Have dessert first," I suggested. I got out of bed and went, not to the little table, but to my jacket. I pulled out my phone and woke it up to take a picture of Grace's face. She didn't realize what I was doing at first.

"What? No, I'm all post-coital," she protested.

"I know, I love it. Look how beautiful you are." I turned the phone around to show her. After a second she shrugged a little, raising her eyebrows. "Yeah, you know it." She laughed. I took another picture. She grabbed the phone and took a couple of pictures of me. She didn't let me see them right away but I had an idea she hadn't zoomed in. "You better not put that on the internet."

"Someone is probably hacking your phone right this second. This'll be all over TMZ in a few minutes." She turned it around to let me see it. *Whoa*, I thought, cracking up because okay, it was a good picture of my face, but yeah, I was completely naked and it was all there. "Don't worry, this will go in my private stash. I know all about computer security now. It's gospel to Jerry and company."

"It's on *my* phone," I pointed out, still snickering. "And I'll let you download it at home, but then I'm deleting it." I turned around to pour the coffee, well aware that she was taking more pictures. I took the coffee over to set it on the bedside table, then went back for the dessert. "Would you cut that out?"

She was giggling. "Nope nope and nope. You started it."

"I wasn't taking full-frontals. But if that's how you want to play, I'll play." I leaned over and got the phone away from her, pulled down the sheet, and took a bunch of pictures as she squealed and tried to hide. Finally I let her pull the sheet up over her head. I sat on the bed to flip through the pictures. "Wow, talk about private stash. Look at all this hotness. You know what, who needs dessert." She laughed again from under the sheet.

Eventually Grace surfaced again, and we had dessert. Talked for a while about our upcoming trip. About the show I had to do before we left, and the character boot camp I was going to have to do the second we got back, and what it all might add up to. I told her again how proud I was of her. What a kick it was going to be to say, my wife is an engineer. Everybody was going to think I was smarter thanks to her. She tried to argue with that, but she kept cracking up.

When we checked out the next morning, it was only the hotel's robust security that kept the press back. I mean, I wasn't a huge celebrity, but there's nothing the gossip sites like better than a morning-after picture. Grace and I looked at each other and smiled. We were both wearing jeans and casual shirts, holding hands and no doubt looking like we hadn't slept much.

I said, "Let's throw them a bone," and she laughed. After the bellhop and the valet got our stuff into the car

I lifted up her left hand and put mine next to it so the rings showed, held the position for a few seconds, then kissed her. That's all we gave them, ignoring all the shouted questions. We got into the car and went back home.

Lucas and Rory's performance was great, of course. The whole show was great, as usual. I could tell Mom was missing the dance life a little bit, and thought maybe, just maybe, she'd start doing some of that again. But it was clear that would be in Minneapolis. Whatever kind of conversation she was having with Dad, he was staying in L.A.

I went in to work for a couple of days that week, to make sure I had all my ducks in a row for when we got back from New Zealand. Jerry took one look at my ring and said, "I knew I liked that guy. Does his look like a bridge, too?"

"More like a wall," I said. "The Great Wall, actually. He's a big guy." Jerry laughed and wished us well.

We took Mom with us to the airport, since she'd decided to leave the same day. Her flight left before ours and from a different terminal, so we kissed and hugged goodbye when we dropped her off, then had the car take us back around the LAX loop. Then it was all the hassle of checking bags, security, finding our gate, and waiting until finally they started boarding. I hadn't paid much attention to the tickets so when Lucas stood up and took my hand, right after the announcement was made, I was surprised. "What?" I said, hurriedly putting my iPad away.

"We're up," he said. I realized he must have gotten us first-class tickets. *Wow*, I thought, but hey: it's a really long flight, and with another twenty-six episodes booked, he could afford it. Plus, of course, there was the movie. And I suspected he had something else cooking.

I had a little something of my own to share. Once we were underway (and provided with champagne) I got my tablet back out and logged into my email. "I thought you might want to see this." I handed it to Lucas, and watched him read the message from Chris.

> Hi Grace, I saw on the news about your wedding. Congratulations, I really mean it.
>
> Thanks for being kind when I stopped by. Thanks to your husband for not breaking my neck. I've been seeing a counselor trying to figure out why I lost my head like that, I think we're getting somewhere.
>
> I noticed you're with Weiss and Associates now. You're going to build great things.
> All the best - Chris

"I never did see him," I said when Lucas looked back up at me. "He wasn't teaching where my stuff was happening. Never contacted me. And I had other fish to fry."

"Plus it hasn't been that long." He leaned over and kissed me, handing the tablet back.

"I know, right? Seems like forever." I took a sip of champagne, waiting for him to 'fess up with whatever was giving him that sneaky happy look. He was taking his own sweet time. He must have known I knew something was up. I got impatient and nudged him at the wrong moment.

He coughed the champagne out of his windpipe, laughing. "Jeez, Grace, what?"

"What's up, you've got a secret. No me gusta."

He laughed again and got out his own tablet. I waited, still impatiently, while he logged in and retrieved a message, then handed it to me.

Hi Lucas,

I'm hearing back from Andy about the tango training, sounds like you're doing great. Diving right into rehearsals when you get back. Anyway, next month I've booked some studio time for you five guys to work with my music producer, Valerie Benton. She put together an album for Andy and his husband recently, did one for Marco and Cameron Hidalgo last year too.

Valerie asked me to run something by you (and I know you'll want to discuss with your agent). She's seen your show. When she talked to her contact at the record company about the cast album for GCG, she asked them about interest in doing a project with you. Standards with a Latin flair. Apparently they were positive. So if that's something you'd want to investigate, have Raquel contact Valerie. Her v-card is attached. Have a great honeymoon and don't break a leg.

Abrazos - Tanith

"I can see it now," I said. "You're going to be the Mexican Frank Sinatra." Lucas snorted, which set me off, and in a second we were both giggling.

"There's already been that guy," he said after a while. "Maybe I can be the Mexican Dean Martin."

"Uh, okay?" I thought for a moment. "Dino and Tarantula?" That set us off again, to the point that a few minutes later the attendant came by to ask if we needed anything, which didn't help. I explained that we were newlyweds, and there might be more giggling, which made her smile. She offered us more champagne, which we of course accepted.

Then Lucas leaned over to kiss me again. "I really love you," he said. "I'm so glad we met."

"Me too. And me too." I kissed him back. "Can't wait to go to the Emmys with you."

"What are you talking about?"

"Well when that episode gets nominated, they're probably going to ask you to sing. If not there, it'll be the People's Choice or the VMAs." He looked terrified. "What?"

"Ugh, *no*."

"Why?"

"That's, like, huge. Too huge. I never thought of that."

"Oh, you'll be fine. And I promise to actually plan ahead and get a dress." He started laughing again. I leaned over to kiss him again. We spilled some champagne. Then I got serious for a second and said quietly, "You can do anything."

He looked into my eyes and said, "Only with you."

Well, that was a hell of a year. And this was a hell of a way to close it out. I stepped out of our chauffeur-driven car and offered a hand to my wife. She swung her beautiful legs out and stood beside me, smiling up at me for a second before turning to face the red carpet. The mob of press on both sides, the long line of premiere ticket-holders stretching away from the Million Dollar Theater down Broadway.

I wore my gunmetal tux again, this time with the explicit permission of my show runner. Grace couldn't wear Michelle's wedding dress again, because Michelle was wearing it. "I planned better this time, huh," she said, scarlet lips curved in a wicked smile.

"Considering we didn't have a ton of time, you did great," I said. "I mean, even if we had a year, you couldn't do better."

She shot me a look, close to cracking up at my last-minute save. Her dress was the same style as that wedding dress – full-skirted, tea length, 50s casual glam – but in vivid red. Nearly the same red as the carpet, with black embroidery around the hem and neckline, sparkling with black rhinestones. We were planning to go to a post-premiere milonga at Shall We Dance, so her shoes were from Worldtone – black satin dressed up with red rhinestones. I asked around and borrowed an antique-looking necklace so people wouldn't forget to look at Grace's beautiful face. It was only costume jewelry, fake opals and rubies set in flowers of fake gold, but it looked terrific under the lights. The almost-matching opal and ruby earrings were real. She always said she wasn't much of one for jewelry, but her face when she opened the box said something different.

Up ahead we could see the marquee, a big wrap-around reading THE GHOST OF CARLOS CARDEL and, on a second line, WORLD PREMIERE. The entire cast was here. All the crew. Nearly everybody had at least one family member or close friend to cheer them on. It was only a little indie movie, but a big studio picked it up. All of us in the cast were super excited. Even Victor Garcia, who had a new action movie in the can.

Julia and Roger were out there somewhere, waiting their turn to go through the doors. So were my parents. Everyone in the line was cheering and applauding as each group came to a stop for pictures in front of the theater. I was trying to act like I'd done this a hundred times.

Tanith promised we'd each get copies of the giant-sized character posters featured on the street-side barricade. I didn't look much like Elvis in mine: hair slicked back, narrow mustache, in a 1930s suit. This character wasn't much like me, either. If the movie was even a modest success, people were going to look at me a whole new way.

"You're such a movie star," Grace said as we went inside. She gave my arm a squeeze. "Oh, cool! Check this out!" In the middle of the lobby: the scale model ballroom that was photographed for our projected historical sets. All over the wall: behind the scenes photos. Over by the doors into the auditorium: Tanith and her fiancé Sid, smiling, waving us on.

"Come on," Tanith said. "Go get your swag bag, find a good seat. Somewhere down in front so you can get up on stage for the Q and A. Damn, Grace, that dress is a knockout."

"Thanks! Guess who made it for me?"

"Uh, hmm, could it be a Matsumoto? Yeah, I thought so."

"I like yours too." Grace stood back and eyed my director, who was wearing a short, tailored, sleeveless matte-black dress with satin lapels over tall black high-heeled boots. "Go-go assassin."

Sid cracked up. I looked at the ceiling, biting my lip. Tanith heaved a very dramatic sigh, rolled her eyes, and pointed inside. "That way." I wrapped my arm around Grace and obeyed directions. Down in the gap between seating and stage, we found all my co-stars and other key components of the movie, milling around, gossiping, catching up. Most of us had seen each other in October for the rough-cut screening, but not since. We had to be forcibly redirected to seats when it came time to start the show.

First came a dance from two of the stars of this movie, which blew my mind a little. We all did good dance work on this thing, but Vicky and Tomás were amazing. Somebody a few rows back said "Holy shit!" when they burst into motion. Plus they were dancing to my recording of 'Cuesta Abajo,' which I couldn't help thinking sounded awfully good. Once the applause tapered off, there was a brief introduction from one of Victor's co-stars on 'L.A. Vice.'

And then, finally, it started. I tried not to squeeze Grace's hand too hard. The first scene was all of us. Since Tanith was an actor too, I knew she knew what that meant to us. Victor was the biggest name in the cast by far, but for those crucial opening minutes, we were all equals. We all had dialogue, Marco and I were playing our guitars, and in a few minutes we'd all be dancing. Showing the world what we could do.

The world might just be a little bit surprised. I sure as hell was. From beginning to end, playing someone so unlike myself, holding my own.

"You can do anything," Grace murmured in my ear. I smiled. Turned to kiss her. Then gazed up at the screen again. Couldn't wait to find out if she was right.

THE END

*If you enjoyed TODAY, TOMORROW & FOREVER,
please consider leaving a positive rating or review. It
really helps! Thanks for reading.*

Want more? **A WINNING HAND** and **TAKE A
NOTE** feature more characters involved with 'Behind
the Strip.' Available at Amazon. Discover this world of
romance at www.thelastories.com.

****

Author's Note

The Emerald Ball and the Hollywood DanceSport
Championships are real ballroom competitions that take
place every year in Los Angeles. The Emerald Ball is
organized by Mr. Wayne Eng, whose home base is Las
Vegas. The Hollywood DanceSport Championship
organizers include Ms. Mary Murphy.

'10-31,' 'L.A. Vice,' and 'Behind the Strip' are
fictional TV shows.

Chrome is a Hollywood nightclub which only exists in
my imagination. The Underground Cabaret is a
fictional dance company.

The joke about Dino and Tarantula is inspired by the
Mex-Rock group Tito and Tarantula. The lead singer,
Tito Larriva, has a voice much as I imagine Lucas'
natural voice to be. Basically, combine Mr. Larriva and
Mr. Eddie Nichols of Royal Crown Revue, and you've
got it.

All of the songs referenced in the text are real.

****

About the Author

Alexandra Caluen lives in a small purple house with her husband, a bottle of Laphroaig, a lot of books, and nine pairs of ballroom shoes. She works in patent law and has enough hair for three people.